EMP

ANTEDILUVIAN PURGE

BOOK ONE

S.A. ISON

OTHER BOOKS BY S.A. ISON

BLACK SOUL RISING

INOCULATION ZERO WELCOME TO THE STONE AGE

BOOK ONE

INOCULATION ZERO WELCOME TO THE AGE OF

WAR BOOK TWO

EMP ANTIDELUVIAN FEAR - BOOK TWO

POSEIDON RUSSIAN DOOMSDAY - BOOK ONE

POSEIDON RUBBLE AND ASH - BOOK TWO

THE HIVE A POST-APOCALYPTIC LIFE

EMP PRIMEVAL

PUSHED BACK A TIME TRAVELER'S JOURNAL

BOOK 1

PUSHED BACK THE TIME TRAVELER'S DAUGHTERS

Book 2

EMP DESOLATION

THE LONG WALK HOME

THE VERMILION STRAIN POST-APOCALYPTIC

EXTINCTION

THE MAD DOG EVENT

DISTURBANCE IN THE WAKE

OUT OF TIME AN OLD FASHION WESTERN

NO ONE'S TIME

A BONE TO PICK

THE WILDER SIDE OF Z

THE WILDER SIDE OF RAGE

THE WILDER SIDE OF FURY

THE WILDER SIDE OF WAR

THE WILDER SIDE OF HELL

ANCIENT DEATH

FOR MY MOTHER AND FATHER

You taught me many things in my life; one of the most important was how to be color blind. Thank you.

♥

FOR MY GRANDPARENTS ON BOTH SIDES

They were true Kentuckians

CHAPTER ONE

Hieronymus Banks pulled into the big box store, watching out for the elderly customers that seemed to inhabit the place. His Peapot, or grandfather, had sent him on several errands. He'd only been home a week, on terminal leave from the Army, and had come to Beattyville, Kentucky, a small coal mining town nestled in the foothills and mountains near the Daniel Boone National Forest. It was still rural, but had crept into the new millennium over the last twenty years.

His twin sister, Willene, had urged him to take his terminal leave there. She'd said their grandfather was very ill. Harry had planned to spend most of his leave in Baden-Württemberg in Germany, where he'd been stationed for the last two years at Stuttgart Army Airfield. He'd wanted to spend his time with his girlfriend, Franziska Gnodtke, a nurse he'd met on base. They'd dated now for well over a year, and Harry was sure she was the one.

So, at his sister's insistence, he'd flown home, and Franziska promised to follow as soon as her visa was updated. This gave Harry a little time to look for a ring. When she arrived, he would propose. He hadn't told Willene, but he was sure his sister would like Franziska. Willene was a nurse too, and he knew the pair would have a lot in common.

Willene had teased him mercilessly about his girl friends when they were younger. Beattyville was a small town, but spread out into the mountains, boasting a population nearing two thousand. Those in the mountains refused to answer the census, so there could be a few more hidden among the hills.

Harry pushed the wide cart down the extensive aisles, looking for the fifty-pound bags of rice. His grandfather had given him a list. He shook his head as he reread the list; it just didn't make any sense. His grandfather had gone on and on about Dr. Peter Vincent Pry, the Executive Director of the Task Force on National and Homeland Security.

"I've been readin' a lot 'bout Dr. Pry, and it's passable interesting, Dr. Pry was also Director of the U.S. Nuclear Strategy Forum, both Congressional Advisory Boards, and he served on the Congressional EMP Commission. Reckon that's what's important here," Peapot had said.

His grandfather had then given him an extensive list. He'd complained, but Willene told Harry to just get what Peapot wanted and not argue. Their eighty-seven-year-old grandfather had congestive heart failure and wasn't expected to live long. Hospice had started coming to help with his care. Willene did a lot of the care herself, but she had to work too. So, when Harry had come home on leave, he had taken over.

Spotting the rice, he easily hefted two large sacks of rice. Once more, he shook his head. He wondered if his grandfather was in the beginning grips of dementia. But, when sitting with the old man, he seemed reasonably sane and cognizant of his surroundings. "People are surely undoubtedly ignorant and Dr. Pry been warning the government bout EMPs and our country's failin' and fragile infrastructure. Congress

7

ain't listening, but I am." His grandfather had then giggled like a little boy caught at some mischief, his eyes disappearing into deep creases.

Harry laughed at his grandfather, who'd always had a mischievous side to him. Willene also seemed to demonstrate that trait. She'd played practical jokes on him when they were kids.

The store had aisles of dried food stuff, boxed foods, and supplies. It was almost like culture shock, seeing all this. In Germany, as in many other countries, they didn't have these kinds of stores. It constantly left him kind of off balance when he came home from overseas; he had to get used to new things.

Looking down, he saw that he needed four, twenty pounds of flour, two, twenty pounds of sugar and three, twenty-five-pound bags of steel cut oats. There was also coffee on the list, and a couple books by Dr. Pry. *Electric Armageddon: Civil-Military preparedness for an Electromagnetic Pulse Catastrophe* and *Apocalypse Unknown: The Struggle to Protect America From an Electromagnetic Pulse Catastrophe.*

He'd gone through the book section twice but couldn't find either of them. He'd go online later and maybe try to find the books. He wondered what had gotten into his grandfather. Had he been watching too many reality shows? Or had he been on the computer looking up things, maybe scaring himself? He just didn't know. His grandfather seemed preoccupied with Dr. Peter Pry and this EMP business.

Harry knew about EMPs and the possible danger from nuclear weapons detonating in the upper atmosphere, causing catastrophic loss of anything not shielded or hardened against an EMP. The Army had educated its people, so Harry was familiar with the basics. He wondered what had spooked his grandfather. Or was this some kind of dementia or brain damage from his health issues?

Harry shook his head. He'd need to swing by the feed store after this stop. Peapot insisted on two hundred pounds of scratch grain for the chickens. When he'd tried to argue that the ten chickens they had didn't warrant that much, his sister punched him on the arm and shook her head, her eyes narrowing into deep brown slits.

"For the Lord in heaven's sakes, just get what he's hankerin' for Harry. You're upsetting him when you fuss," she said.

"But he is wasting money, and what the hell are we going to do with all this stuff? We couldn't eat that much in years," Harry had argued, but took the list and the money, rubbing his arm. His sister had a mean right hook.

"Look, if Peapot wants to buy a pony, we'll get it for him, I don't care. He doesn't have much time left and I don't want him to fuss with anyone 'bout his whims," she'd said, her mouth set at the same mulish tilt as his own.

It had broken his heart to see Peapot so weak and so unbelievably frail. It'd been over three years since he'd seen him last. Back then, he'd been robust and healthy, going on long walks around their property. Now, he was shrunken and pale gray.

9

Their family lineage in these mountains was long, laced with Cherokee and Creek, as well as Scots Irish. His great-great-grandfather and great-grandfather had both lived to be well over one hundred years old. He took after the Scots Irish with a hint of native American, while Willene took on more of the Cherokee and Creek connection. Her skin was darker, as were her deep brown eyes.

Harry had been told by his grandfather that their unique eye colors were due to dual spirits. Their eye colors went back generations, and he and Peapot sported the brown and hazel eye colors. Now, his grandfather's rheumy eyes were faded, and he was deteriorating fast. He was glad Willy had insisted he come home.

Pulling down the tailgate of the old 1978 Dodge pickup, Harry tossed the sacks of rice, oats and other purchases onto the rusted bed. Peapot owned the old truck for as long as Harry could remember. He shook his head in wonderment that the damn thing still ran.

Peapot had taught Harry how to fix the truck, and they'd spent hours in old junk yards searching for old truck parts when he was a teen. Harry suspected that the activity had largely kept him out of trouble and where his grandfather could keep an eye on him.

In the old barn, back up a ways from the house, were shelves that lined the far wall. Neatly kept, they were stacked with old truck parts. Harry wondered if his grandfather had become a hoarder, but the neatness of it all made him doubt it.

10

After stopping by the feed store, he swung over to a local beer hall, The Lazy J, on Broadway to get a drink. It was hot and getting late in the day. When he got home, Willene would have him out in the garden picking weeds, so he wanted something refreshing before he headed home to do that.

When he was a kid, he'd hated picking weeds; a tedious task for a busy kid. But now, it left him tranquil. He enjoyed the quiet, and the soft clucking of the chickens nearby. He'd made a stool just for that purpose, to sit and pull the many weeds that seemed to spring up overnight.

He went up to the bar counter, looking around. He groaned internally when he saw Earl Bayheart. He and Earl had grown up together and had even been friends. But when they'd gotten to high school, their friendship had cooled, so much so that there had been several fist fights between them. Nothing serious, just boys letting off steam over a girl.

When Harry had signed up for the Army, he'd tried to talk Earl into going with him on the buddy system. Earl had laughed and said he'd not be a slave in the U.S. military. Everybody knew that soldiers ended up as *cannon fodder*. He was going to work in the mines like his daddy and his granddaddy.

That life had taken its toll on Earl. The man looked ten years older than Harry and was missing a leg. Harry heard years ago that it had been in a mining accident. Coal mines were dangerous places, almost as dangerous as Fallujah or Afghanistan.

In Beattyville, there wasn't much in the way of job opportunities; you were either a farmer, coal miner, logger, or military. There was also moonshine, and that too was dangerous, and now also Harry had heard about meth labs in the mountains.

Harry wanted to see the world, and he had, in his twenty years of service. But he'd spent too many years in Afghanistan, Iraq, Syria, and other hotspots. He'd seen too much death and evil to want to stay longer. He considered himself lucky not to have been shot or blown up. Younger men were taking his place. For now, he was looking forward to a quiet beer.

It was not to be. Earl sauntered over to him, a cigarette hanging with irreverent neglect off his lip. Every time Harry came back, it was the same ritual. He should have known. It'd been three years, and still things hadn't changed.

He supposed he'd changed over the years. It wouldn't have been so bad, but Earl seemed like he hadn't grown up. Especially after the accident in the mine that took his leg. Earl had been more easygoing than he had, when they were kids. He sipped his beer, waiting for Earl's first volley.

"Where ya been, Banks? Back from war? You're a sight for sore eyes." Earl sniggered, scratching at his brown patchy beard, his homely face bright.

"Hmm," Harry replied noncommittally.

"That all you got for a friend? I ain't seen you in a coon's age. What in the Sam hill you been up to?" Earl continued, settling into his rhythm of good-natured harassment. "Why, I was even gonna share some chaw

12

with ya or maybe a snort." He grinned, showing stained teeth and several missing upper and lower incisors.

Harry took another sip of his beer and turned and smiled at Earl, his own teeth brilliant white and straight, and more importantly, all there. His eyes, one brown and one hazel, crinkled into mischievous triangles of humor. He noted that Earl's smile slowly left his face as his upper lip curled over the stained teeth, as though trying to hide them from sight. Harry knew it was mean-natured, but both men always tried to dig into each other. Harry guessed it was a guy thing.

"I reckon that's mighty nice, but I'm afraid I don't chaw. Nothing against ya. Reckon I'd better be scootin' on home. Willy will be wondering after me," he said in the heavy Appalachian speak. He'd lost most of his accent when he'd gone into the army. But when home, he fell back into its habit from time to time, like now, either on purpose or unintended.

He got up and started for the door. He could hear Earl's uneven footsteps behind and knew the man was following him out of the building. He hoped Earl wasn't brewing for a long conversation, as he really did need to get home. There were always things to do when he was home, and sometimes he wondered how his sister and his grandfather ever got things accomplished.

Getting into the old Dodge, Harry turned the ignition, the engine rumbling to life. He adjusted himself in the cracked leather seats and pulled the old seatbelt across, clicking it.

"Harry? How many folks you kill?" Earl asked somberly.

Harry didn't look at him, looking instead out the windshield. Then he spoke softly. "Too many, Earl." He lifted his hand slightly in farewell and drove away, not looking back.

Earl watched Harry pull away, his hand idly scratching at his skin. He pulled the cigarette out of his mouth, spat, and took a long puff. He couldn't figure Harry out. Life had been so much easier when they'd been kids and had played in the creek and fished and chased lightning bugs. But all that changed as they'd gotten older.

Earl had envied Harry. Harry had a sister, and a mother, grandfather and grandmother that had loved him, though Harry's mom and grandmother died too young. Earl's father had been a lazy drunk, like his grandfather. He hadn't understood when he was a young'un, but as he grew older he began to realize how different their families were. As a teen, he was embarrassed by his family, and shame seemed to follow him.

Life had been hard in his home, and as Earl had grown older, more and more responsibilities had been heaped on his shoulders. He'd wanted to go with Harry into the Army but had been afraid. Afraid to leave the mountains and all he knew. Afraid to leave his drunk of a father. Afraid to know a world different from his own. And so over the years, he'd watched and listened to Harry as he came home, telling of different places, people, and customs.

It all seemed like a fairytale, but Earl knew it was all true. He did, after all, watch TV. And as he and his friends grew older, they drank together and worked in the coal mine. Many of his friends had become ill from the coal dust and deplorable working conditions; Harry came home, strong, tall, and fit. It was as though living here in the mountains had sucked away Earl's life.

Though he'd quit the mine after the accident, and become a mechanic, the damage had been done. Earl puffed once more on the cigarette and tossed it to the gutter, then walked back into the bar for another beer. He liked Harry and Willene; they were two of the best people he knew. He just wished he'd gone with Harry that day, into the Army.

Harry sat hunched over the bed, holding his grandfather's hand. He was sitting in a hard-oak chair, with a cushion his mother made years before. He held nail clippers and clipped gently away at the thick horny nails. He could feel his grandfather's eyes on him.

"What is it, Peapot? Am I hurting your hand?" Harry asked gently, squeezing the old hand tenderly.

"Naw, was just thinking," the old man said, his voice sounding thin and weak.

"'Bout what?" Harry asked, clipping a little more, his gaze darting up to his grandfather from time to time.

"'Bout the cave. You been down there lately?" he asked.

"No sir, not for some years. You shouldn't be going down there anymore. Willy told me that you

15

been sneakin' down there. She said that's what set you off this time," Harry chided gently.

The cave, located on their property was a place of wonder and security. It had been a secret of their family for many generations. During the world wars, during the depression, during strife, it had been a place to go. It had also been one of the greatest playgrounds a child could have.

"You and your sissy should go down for a visit. Make her go; she won't go with me," the old man grouched.

"Peapot, you know girls don't like to go into dark old caves when they get to be women. Just boys like us." Harry grinned and squeezed the hand he was holding. He paused and looked down at the old hand, so fragile, the veins blue and roping along the knuckles and large dark freckles and age spots.

When had his skin gotten so thin and papery? When had his strong grandfather gotten so old? Harry swallowed and kept his eyes down, blinking away the sheen of tears. The memories of his strong, robust grandfather had been replaced by this feeble, shrunken man.

"It's near time. You need ta go to that cave," the old man insisted, his body restless and fidgeting.

"What's near time, Peapot? And why do we need to go to the cave?" Harry asked, wondering why the old man was so adamant about him taking Willene down to the cave. His heart fluttered with the fear, knowing that his grandfather was so weak and may be dying right before him.

16

He and his sister used to play for hours down in the cave, exploring. Over the last one hundred years, modifications had been made to the cavern, each generation adding their own touches. There were many *rooms*, some large and cathedral-like, some small and closet-like.

Each of the rooms was filled with things the children loved and cherished: books, toys, lanterns, flashlights, beds, couches, and even a toilet and fireplace. The children had been shown how a fire could be built and had been, on the homemade hearth and grate positioned by the deep crack that actually pulled the smoke out of the cave. Their grandfather explained that there was suction via the crack and drew it through the rock and filtered out of the cave at some point. They had marveled at it and run in and out of the cave, looking for the smoke from the fire. They'd never found it. The fireplace kept the cave warm. In the summer the caves were cool and, in the winter, they were warm and snug. It was the go-to place for fun, though only the children played there.

His grandfather looked out the window, not answering, and again Harry wondered if his grandfather was mentally there in the room with him. But his eyes seemed clear and he didn't appear confused. He heard the door, and Willene answered it downstairs. Marilyn's voice drifted up the stairs. She was the hospice nurse.

"Marilyn's here, Peapot. She'll be up in a few minutes," Harry said, putting the clippers down and patting the shriveled hand lovingly. He bent forward and kissed his grandfather's head.

"She'll be good for you," his grandfather said, and smiled knowingly.

Harry looked confused, and worried about his grandfather once more. He went to the radio to turn down the volume when the power went out. Pulling his hand back, he looked at the silent radio, cocking his dark head to the side. *Uh oh*, he thought. That's not good and looked back at his grandfather. A soft smiled flitted across his face. It was good to see him, but not like this. His heart flipped.

CHAPTER TWO

"Power's out," Willene called unnecessarily from the bottom of the stairs.

"Yeah, I got that," Harry called back, and turned to his grandfather, who was smiling still, his eyes closed.

When Marilyn came up the stairs, she smiled at Harry and he smiled back in reflex. He'd known Marilyn all his life. She was a few years younger than him, but he'd gone to school with her. She had a son, he knew, but her husband, Moses, had died in the coal mines some years back. Her boy was six or seven, he believed.

"He seems a little disoriented today. I'm not sure what that is about," Harry said, laying a hand lightly on Marilyn's forearm.

Marilyn's dark eyes shone with an inner radiance, and she smiled. "Well, we'll just see how he's doin', won't we." She moved past Harry and into the room with his grandfather.

Marilyn Little watched as Harry left the room, his broad shoulders filling the doorway as he walked out. He was a tall man and well made. She smiled. She'd liked Harry since they were children. He had a sweetness about him. Perhaps she'd loved him. She didn't really know.

They'd all been friends since grade school, and she and Willene were as close as two peas in a pod. Though a few years younger than Willene, they'd hung out on the swing sets and monkey bars. Willene had at times, carried the much smaller child, as though guarding her. Marilyn had tagged along, and they'd remained best friends since.

Since they'd grown up, Harry was gone for years at a time, but he was still as handsome as ever with his thick dark hair and beautiful, oddly-colored eyes. They were hypnotic, though when she was young, she'd not really noticed. She'd had a crush on Harry in her freshman year in high school. Like most boys, he'd been oblivious.

She'd married her high school sweetheart, Moses Little, and had been happy. After numerous attempts at getting pregnant and many failures, they'd given up. But then, eight years ago, she'd gotten pregnant, and she and Moses had been thrilled. When she'd been seven months along, there'd been an accident in the mine and Moses had been killed.

Had it not been for Willene, she might well have lost the baby. Willene had moved her into the farmhouse until she'd delivered Monroe. He was a sweet baby and she'd been smitten. He'd brought her untold joy, and also sorrow that Moses would not see his son grow up.

Up until that point Marilyn had been a housekeeper, but Willene had encouraged her to go to nursing school, and had even helped, along with other nurses and even Peapot, take care of Monroe while she went to school. Since then, she'd worked as a nurse and part-time as a hospice nurse. Monroe was a happy healthy child.

20

She felt as though the Banks family was her own. She loved the old man, and he had become a surrogate grandfather for Monroe. Moses had also been an only child, and by the time he'd died, his parents had passed away some years before. Her own parents had long since moved to Lexington, and she saw them every few months.

"How are you feeling today, Mr. Banks?" Marilyn asked, smiling down at the old man.

"Oh, fine as a frog's hair." He gave a gummy grin and wheezed out a laugh.

"Well, that's awfully fine then, isn't it?" She laughed and patted his hand.

Harry went downstairs and joined his sister in the kitchen. She was breading chicken to fry on the gas stove. There was flour smudged on her face and flour all over the counters. He wasn't sure how his sister did it, but she always seemed to make a mess, no matter the task at hand. She was a wonderful cook, but messy as hell. She liked to say it was the artist in her.

The cast iron frying pan popped a little, ready for the chicken. It sat on the huge old-fashioned cast iron wood stove. Over the years, the stove had been partially converted to gas. The wood usage part of the stove was still used in the winter, but during the warmer seasons, the gas burners were used. It had been in the family since the old farmhouse was built in 1878.

"Can I help?" Harry asked, walking over to the refrigerator and opening the door. It was dark inside.

21

"Keep that door closed or you'll let the cold out. And no. Just sit here and keep me company," Willene said as she salted the raw chicken, then peppered it. She then dipped the pieces into beaten eggs, then flour, then back to the egg mixture and then to corn meal and then into the cast iron frying pan. A satisfying sizzle erupted from the pan, and the scent of fried chicken filled the air, causing Harry's stomach to rumble.

"Yes ma'am," Harry said, his eyes crinkling in good humor, and reached a finger over to the chocolate cake that was sitting on the counter. He ran the tip of his finger along the bottom edge, catching some of the homemade chocolate frosting. He brought it up to his mouth and rolled his eyes back in bliss.

He missed the down-home cooking that he could only get here. Franziska could cook, but not like this. He hoped Willene would teach her some tricks while she was here. He still hadn't told Willene about Fran, or that she was coming. Maybe tonight, after dinner.

"Don't you ruin your appetite. I'll scald you," Willene said, a dark brow rising and her eyes narrowing, a smile pulling at the side of her mouth.

Harry grinned, "That's a mess of chicken you're frying. You need me to shuck taters?" He snuck another swipe of the icing. He jerked his hand away as his sister took a swipe at him with the long fork she used to turn the chicken.

"Marilyn and her boy are stayin' for supper. This is her last call of the day, so I figured we'd feed them up," Willene said, turning her back and moving the frying chicken around in the cast iron skillet. The sizzling and popping of the chicken filled the air.

"Monroe is here?" Harry asked, looking around as though the child would pop out of the cabinet.

"He's outside playin' with Charley," Willene said. Charley was the family dog, a King Charles Spaniel. Harry had gotten him for Willene for their birthday.

"Guess I'll go keep him company since you don't need my help," he said and ambled out of the house.

"That's fine. I'll just shuck them taters myself, brother," Willene yelled after him, a laugh in her voice.

Harry could hear the boy laughing, and found him chasing the dog as they came running from around the house. Harry walked onto the long wide porch and sat in the porch swing. There were also several old wooden rocking chairs and two gliders spread around. It was room for plenty of company.

The house didn't have air conditioning, but it was high enough in the mountains to stay relatively cool in the summer months, especially at night. The windows were open to the constant breeze and strategic placement of fans helped move the air around. Sitting out on the porch ensured a relaxing and enjoyable pastime.

He watched the child and dog run up and down the hill in front of the house. The farmhouse sat nestled five hundred feet up from the road atop a medium steep hill, in one hundred acres of forested land. It had been cut over the years for its timber, but recently had been left to grow. Down the hill were two huge black walnut trees that obscured the house from the road, and apple trees dotted their way up the hill toward the house.

When he and his sister were children, they had run and played up and down the hill until well after dark, and climbed the walnut and apple trees. When the trees were loaded with fruit, they'd sat among the branches and eaten their fill. They'd chased ladybugs, June bugs, and lightning bugs. They'd rolled from the top of the hill all the way down to the bottom, running back up for another go.

A smile gently curved his mouth as he watched Monroe do the same thing, knowing the child would be covered with grass stains. Neither his mother nor grandfather had ever cared that he and his sister came in filthy every night after playing on the hill. He was sure Monroe would be filthy as well. No one cared; he'd sleep soundly tonight.

Charley barked and followed the child down the hill, falling down a few times and rolling along beside him. There was a cool breeze blowing and it felt good. The twilight was quiet except for the childish laughter that drifted back up the hill. He heard the screen door open and close, and looked over as Marilyn made her way to the swing.

"How is he?" Harry asked, concern in his voice. She looked worried.

Marilyn's dark eyes gazed up from her phone, and her eyes cleared. "He's as well as can be expected. He's comfortable and in no pain, and seems very lucid. I'm sorry to say, though, he hasn't more than a week. His blood pressure is lower, as is his pulse, but he isn't

24

in any distress and he isn't sufferin'," she said and smiled softly, compassion glowing in her eyes.

"Oh, okay. It was just that you looked worried," Harry said.

"Oh that? No, it's just my phone died. I know I charged it, but it's dead," she said, handing Harry her phone.

Harry took her phone and tried to power it up. Nothing. He didn't have a cellphone as he wasn't in country enough to have one. He called to Willene to check her phone.

A few minutes later, Willene came to the screen door and looked at her brother. "Mine's dead. I checked the house phone and it's dead too."

"Well that's normal. The power is out," Harry said.

"No. It's a landline. Even if the power is out, that line is always active," Willene said.

"Maybe I'll take a trip into town and see what's going on." Harry got up from the swing. Marilyn made to get up, but Harry placed a hand gently on her shoulder. He noticed a soft blush on her smooth light brown skin. "Don't worry. You sit and relax, I'll go and check things out." He smiled at both women and made his way around the house. "Don't forget the taters," Harry called back, laughing. Monroe was hot on his heels, chattering away.

"Peckerwood!" Willene's voice drifted around the house and he heard both women cackle with loud laughter. He sniggered in response.

Willene went back into the kitchen and turned the frying chicken down to low. She'd let it fry slowly to ensure a crispy crust and cooked interior. She gathered up some potatoes and placed them in a bowl, grabbed a dish towel, threw that over her shoulder and went out to the porch.

She sat beside Marilyn on the porch swing and began to peel potatoes.

"Would you like me to do that for you, Willy?" Marilyn asked.

"Naw, I've got it. The chicken will take some time to fry, so figured I'd get these potatoes on."

She began cutting the clean potatoes with a small paring knife, her favorite knife for cutting up veggies. The breeze felt good on her face; it got hot in the kitchen when using the stove, gas or wood. She watched as her grandfather's truck headed down the hill and grinned, knowing Monroe would be good company for him.

She worried that her brother was way too serious these days. He'd always been a serious boy, and had grown into an even more serious man. But she also knew he needed a little youthful joy in his life. Monroe was a little talker, and she laughed at the thought of him chatting away to Harry.

"What's so funny?" Marilyn asked.

"I was thinking about Harry driving all the way to town with Monroe talking his ear off," Willene said, laughing once more.

Marilyn joined in, and both women watched the truck disappear around the mountain curve.

26

"It sure is good to have Harry home," Marilyn said.

Willene cut her eyes to the side and smiled. She knew Marilyn liked Harry very much. She'd known pretty much all her life. Whenever Harry had come home, she'd made sure to have Marilyn over for dinners and visits.

"What?" Marilyn asked defensively.

"Nothing. I need to get these taters in the water to boil. I'll be back out in a bit. Relax and enjoy the breeze." Willene laughed and winked at her friend, then took the bowl of potatoes back into the house. She knew she shouldn't tease Marilyn, but she couldn't help it. Perhaps she would do a little matchmaking with her brother. After all, he wasn't getting any younger. Marilyn was good people and Monroe needed a daddy. Why not Harry? She laughed softly to herself and shook her head.

CHAPTER THREE

Monroe came running up behind him as he reached the truck. "Momma told me I can come wiff you," Monroe said, a wide grin on his light brown face, a front tooth missing.

Harry grinned back and helped the boy into the truck. He grabbed the boy's head and squeezed it, making silly noises. The child's peals of laughter filled the truck cab. He helped Monroe buckle in, and then pulled out and down the long drive.

As he drove, a few old cars passed him. There were numerous cars sitting in the middle of the road. He listened absently as Monroe chattered like a magpie and answered him just as absently. The child never noticed. He grinned. Monroe's hands were in constant motion and his feet were kicking back and forth, his head waggling side to side as he spoke.

Harry carefully and slowly wound his way around the stalled vehicles, coming to stop by a small compact car. A man was standing by the engine with the hood of the vehicle up, scratching his balding head with one hand, a rag held in the other.

"What seems to be the matter?" Harry called.

"Damn if I'd know, doggone thang's stopped on me," the man said puzzled.

"Need a lift?" Harry offered.

"Naw, my house is down yonder a bit. I can push it easy. Thanks kindly." He bent once more to look down.

"Say, does your phone work?" Harry asked, suspicion creeping up his spine. Small tendrils of fear

28

began to wiggle out and swim about his body, like tadpoles set free.

The man dug in his pocket and pulled out his phone. He looked down, pressed a button, shook it, pressed more on the buttons, shook it again as though that would fix it, and looked up confused, shaking his head. He shrugged his shoulders and put it back into his pocket, then leaned back over and looked down into his car.

Harry just shook his head and pulled away, and then drove up the road and past a convenience store. Several people were at the pumps, yelling and shaking their fists. Others were coming out of the store and gathering around. He pulled off the road, turned off the truck's engine, and listened.

Ж

Officer Clay Patterson was driving back from Lexington to Beattyville along Highway 52. He'd had a court date to testify against a meth suspect. He and Brian, his partner, a German shepherd mix, stopped off for lunch at a BBQ joint. It was small and popular. Once back in Beattyville, he would stop by the precinct to finish up paperwork and then head home.

Some of the curves were forcing him to drive slowly. Brian was a stoic dog when out on the road. Clay had named him after his first partner, who'd been killed in the line of duty years ago. Clay had gotten a police dog, Hugo, several years ago, in lieu of a human partner, but unfortunately Hugo could not take the curves in the mountains and low valleys. Poor Hugo threw up whenever they left Beattyville. He'd had to rehome the dog to the Lexington airport, where they could use him.

He'd then gotten Brian two years ago and the dog had an iron stomach. Brian looked over at him and grinned, his tongue hanging out. Clay reached over and petted the canine. He slowed down once more for a sharp curve when his police cruiser just stopped running; the vehicle shut down, along with the power steering.

"Well Swanee! What the hell? What is goin' on?" Clay cried out as the cruiser edged toward the fall off. Pulling as hard as he could, the wheels turned toward the mountain and the cruiser finally came to a stop. He opened the door and climbed out, his heart racing, his breaths coming in pants.

"Come on Brian, get out an' come sit over yonder," he called the dog out of the car and indicated the far side of the road. He pulled his smart phone out and tried to call the station. He stared at the blank screen. He turned his phone off and then back on. Nothing.

He then pressed the mic on his utility vest, trying to raise the station. He was unsure if there would be a signal with the mountains all around. Clicking the mic, he heard nothing. Not even static.

"Shit," he muttered. He looked up and down the mountain road. He could hear no other vehicles. He walked over and locked the cruiser, then called Brian to him. "Like as not, looks like we are walkin' home, boy."

Walking to the trunk, he opened it. Inside was a backpack. He put several bottles of water inside it. He also took some flares and put them in the bag.

He checked his heavy steel flashlight. It was bright, so in it went. There was a small med kit in the pack, as well as sanitary wipes. He pulled out a plastic bag of dog chow, some protein bars and beef jerky, three fruit cups, and Brian's food bowl. He placed all these in the backpack.

He drank down two bottles of water and put the empties back into the trunk. He also rolled up an emergency blanket and stuffed it into the pack.

He looked around once more, hoping against hope that someone would drive by. Huffing, he hoisted the backpack over his shoulder and began to walk toward Beattyville, Brian walking obediently beside him.

Ж

It was quiet, unnaturally quiet. Harry looked in the air and saw the contrails of planes, but no planes. There weren't that many flying over usually, but still. If this was what he thought, then all those planes were down now, crashed, on fire, and thousands were dead. Harry swallowed hard. His lips trembled, and he bit down on them.

"Whassa matter, Mr. Harry?" Monroe asked, his small voice filling the cab of the truck.

"Not sure, Monroe, but let's drive a bit more. Okay?" he said. He looked down at the child and winked.

He drove along the streets and maneuvered around stalled cars and trucks. People were out in the streets, talking and looking around. A few waved at him and went back to talking. Harry weaved around and pulled through, then turned and drove through the small shopping mall and made his way back home. He felt numb. He knew what it was, but didn't want to believe it.

It was a clear day and it was pretty out, not a cloud in the sky so no thunderstorms or tornados, yet everything was down. He decided to drive a different route home, and everywhere he looked people were coming out of their homes or businesses, their body language clearly saying something was wrong.

EMP was screaming in his brain. His grandfather had wanted the books and had been talking about Dr. Peter Vincent Pry. All that interest, and the innuendoes about things coming.

Then his heart shattered. Franziska! He'd never see her again. A sob choked him, but he swallowed it down. His eyes cut over to Monroe, who was looking out the window. He didn't want to upset the child. He looked out the window in turn, blinking rapidly.

His world had just shrunk down to a day's walk, and within hours or days all hell would break loose. He had to get home and prepare. He hit the accelerator, a primal urge to get back home nearly overwhelmed him.

Glancing at Monroe, he knew the child and his mother would need to stay with them. Monroe didn't know his father, he'd been killed before his birth, and Marilyn had no one to protect her and her son. They'd be targets for anyone who wanted what they had, even if it wasn't much. He also knew that, as pretty as

Marilyn was, she would become a target for men bent on rape.

Arriving home, he pulled up and saw his sister and Marilyn sitting on the swing, sipping tea. Monroe exited the truck and immediately ran after Charley. The two went tumbling down the hill in front of the house. Harry came up to the women, his face serious. They both stopped talking.

"What's wrong, Harry?" Willene asked, concerned.

"I think I know what has happened, I think we've been hit with an EMP, an electromagnetic pulse. The thing is, I don't know how it happened. When I left Germany, there was no intel that indicated an immediate threat. Scientists have been talking about coronal emissions for years now, but nothing on the news has indicated an imminent threat. If it was a solar emission, that could mean that it may well be worldwide."

"But, what does that mean to us? I don't understand," Marilyn said, her dark eyes beginning to fill with fear.

"An EMP can take out all systems that are electrical, that means computers, satellites, electrical grids, along with all banking, medical and so on. If it has a computer chip or if it is connected to or needs electricity, it will no longer work. If it is an enemy that has done this, they've detonated a nuclear device above the ground, which means some kind of nuclear fallout. Not knowing where detonations may have occurred, or even if they've occurred, is something we can't worry about."

Harry ran his fingers through his hair, making it stand up on end. He paced up and down the porch, then looked out over the valley below him. "Thank God we don't have nuclear power plants. Those will become unstable, and if they don't have backup generators online, then you can count on nuclear meltdowns wherever they are."

"What should we do?" Willene asked, her hand grasping one of Marilyn's.

"Marilyn, I need to take you home an' pack up everything you and Monroe will need for the foreseeable future. I'll drive you there and help. You'll need to also pack up all the food in your house, fridge, freezer, cupboards, everything. Also, all toiletries you have. Do you have any weapons?" Harry asked.

"Moses had a gun, but I think it is still up in the closet. I never took it out," Marilyn said, clearly numbed from shock. "Why can't I take my car? Why do I have to leave my home?"

"Your car is too new, it is probably fried. You can try it, but I don't think it will work. Within a few days or even hours, the world is going to go sideways. You and Monroe will be vulnerable, and you'll become a target for what you have in your home. You'll also become a target for ruthless men," he said as he helped her up from the swing. He could feel the tremors in her hand.

"What do you need me to do, Harry?" Willene asked, also rising.

"Go pull out everything from the fridge you can process in the canning jars. There isn't going to be any more food preservation unless we dehydrate it, smoke it, or can it. Also, I'm going up to my room to get my Glock; you'll need to go down to the basement and see what kind of handguns Peapot has in the gun safe. Keep one on you at all times from now on."

Marilyn called Monroe to her and told him to go into the house and eat dinner. She kissed him on the head and said she'd be back with Mr. Harry in a while. Harry went to his room. He'd not put his weapons in the gun safe but had kept his door locked, he'd been so busy running errands for Peapot that he'd not thought about it. He put the Glock in a shoulder holster and put a light jacket on over. He put a spare magazine in the pocket of his jacket. He didn't think he'd need it, but wanted it.

Harry looked in on his grandfather and saw that he was asleep. A soft smile curved on his lips and he turned and headed downstairs.

He met Marilyn by the truck.

"My car doesn't work, Harry," she said to him, her hand on the passenger side door.

Harry shook his head and they both got in. They drove down the hill and headed to her small apartment complex, twenty-five miles down the road in town. When they arrived, there were people out in the street, most of them relaxed and talking.

He pulled into the apartment complex's parking area and Marilyn hopped out. He was about to follow her up to her apartment when he heard his name being called. Turning around, he saw Earl limping toward him. He groaned internally. He really didn't have time for this. He nodded Marilyn on and told her he'd join her in a moment.

"Harry, can I talk to ya for a minute?" Earl asked, all sarcastic derision gone from his homely face.

"Sure Earl, what do you need?" Harry asked.

"Harry, something bad is goin' on. Nothin' works and everything gone ta rack an' ruin. I gotta bad, bad, feelin'," Earl said quietly, his blue eyes flitting around him, ensuring he wasn't overheard.

Harry looked at Earl, studying his face carefully. Though the two had had an odd relationship, there'd never been any hard feelings. He made a decision and hoped he wouldn't regret it.

"You know what an EMP is?" Harry asked quietly, looking around as well to make sure no one heard them.

Earl blanched, his face draining of all color. Harry knew the man in front of him understood and was coming to grips with the awful truth.

"Is your home safe, Earl? Do you have enough food? Do you have a weapon and ammo?" Harry asked.

"I live in a trailer park, and all I got is some canned food an' beer. I got a deer rifle and .38 special. I got a little ammo," he said, shame flooding his face, red splotches suffused his cheeks.

"Go get all your food, any medications, toiletries, clothes, and whatever else you think you might need. Then go to your garage an' get all the gas tanks you can load into the back of your truck, and if you can fill them, fill them. If you have diesel, get that; my truck

36

runs on it. Anything you can think of, bring it to my house. Tell Willy I told you that you are to stay with us."

Earl's eyes sheened with unshed tears, and his mouth worked a bit before he could speak. "Thank you, Harry, I'm obliged to ya an' I won't let you down. I'll bring everything I can find," Earl's voice trembled with emotion, bringing a lump to Harry's throat.

CHAPTER FOUR

Harry studied the man before him. Life was going to be difficult and they would need more bodies to protect them. "Earl, do you know anyone you can trust, I mean trust with your very life? That works in the coal mine?" Harry asked.

Earl looked down at his foot and his artificial leg, shuffled it back and forth, scattering gravel. He chewed his lip and then looked at Harry, a smile on his lips.

"Boggy Hines. He's a good feller, he ain't ignorant. He lives a few trailers down from mine. I've known him most of his life. Knew his granny, she was a good woman too. His momma done left outta there when he was a young'un, but his granny raised him right. He keeps to hisself, but a good an' Godly man an' hard worker. Ain't never heard nothin' bad 'bout him an' he's always good ta help a friend out," Earl said.

"Tell Boggy the same thing I've told you, to gather everything he thinks he will need. Also, can you two swing by the mine and pick up dynamite or any explosives you can get your hands on? Be careful and don't let anyone see you two. It's fixin' to get bad soon, say nothing of what you're doing to anyone. We need to get this done now and in secret. Carry a weapon on you and don't let anyone take your truck," Harry said sternly, the soldier's voice coming through.

At Earl's quick nod, Harry turned and went to Marilyn's apartment to help her. He entered into the small apartment and looked around. It was neat as a pin. He saw Monroe's toys in a box. He walked over and took the box and carried it out to the truck. He made sure the lid to the toybox was firmly closed and placed it in the bed of the truck.

Coming back in, he began to open the pantry and cabinets. He was glad he'd grabbed the reusable grocery bags when he'd left the farmhouse. He began to pull everything out of the freezer and refrigerator. He could hear Marilyn in the bedroom pulling things out of the closet.

Between the two of them, it only took an hour to search the apartment for needed items. He'd gone back and forth from the apartment to the truck, loading the bed. He was pleased that Marilyn had an extensive emergency first aid bag. Once everything was thrown into the truck, he and Marilyn double checked that nothing would fly out once they got going. He'd tied down a few of the lighter items, securing them.

People stood around talking and watched their activity, but Harry didn't look back. He kept his head down and hurried. Once they were finished, they got back into the truck. Harry backed out and turned the truck around. He came to a screeching halt as a large man stood in the truck's path.

Marilyn gasped, bringing her hand to her chest, but said nothing. Harry put his hand into his jacket and brought his weapon to his lap, keeping it out of sight.

"Can I help you, mister?" Harry called out the window calmly.

"What you folks doin'? Looks like you runnin' for the hills?" the man asked a little belligerently. He had on a checkered shirt buttoned up to his double chin. His face was red and sweat beaded on top of his balding head.

"How come your piece of shit truck workin'? Mine ain't. That little nigger lady an' you can just stay put, an' you can give me that truck. I got young'uns I need to get yonder to home," he continued, nodding back to six kids standing by a large newer truck.

Harry's nostril's flared, his mouth tightened, and his eyes narrowed as rage flared through his body, the hot lava speeding through his veins. He smelled blood. Then he smiled and glanced at Marilyn, whose face had gone red with anger. He winked at her and then looked back at the large man, whose fists were resting on his wide hips.

"Sorry buddy, can't help you. This here truck doesn't operate with ignorant white trash, bigots, and peckerwoods. You'll have to figure out another way to get your young'uns home." The smile on Harry's face belied the fire in his eyes. His hand tightened over the Glock. He watched as the man's face turned bright red and his double chin began to jiggle with indignation.

The large man started forward, his body gearing up for a fight. Slowly, Harry brought up the Glock, bringing it just high enough for the large man to see. He could feel Marilyn's hand, gentle on his arm in silent caution.

His smile widened as the man stopped abruptly, his eyes going large as they fixed on the weapon pointing at him. The red color drained fast, as though it were a turd flushed away in a toilet. He held his hands up

40

defensively and backed up, getting out of the way of the truck.

Harry looked at Marilyn, whose eyes were large as saucers. He winked again and pulled away.

"It's starting already and it hasn't been more than three hours," Marilyn said, her voice shaking, her hands couldn't seem to stay still and fluttered in her lap.

"This is nothing. It's gonna get a whole lot worse," he said in a low voice, his lips thinning.

"How much worse, Harry? And how long will this last?" Marilyn asked. He caught her wiping tears from her cheeks as his eyes cut over.

"The EMP has essentially taken out all banking, transportation, and communications for starters. That means no more food transported across the country, no more deliveries." He slowed the truck down; there were several people lingering in the road.

"Large older farm equipment will no longer work without fuel because fuel trucks and equipment may not work, and if they aren't old models, their computer components will have fried. Fuel tanks are normally run with electricity. Along with the newer farm equipment having computer chips, so do most trucks, cars and airplanes, trains and so on," Harry said.

"Oh, my gentle Jesus, you mean all those people who were up in planes are dead?" Marilyn said, her voice harsh as she tried to hold back a sob.

"Yes, sadly, they are gone. But their suffering is over. Ours is just beginning. People are soon going to realize that no one is going to come and help them," Harry said, scanning the road.

"You mean the government won't help us? FEMA?" Marilyn asked, dismay lacing her voice.

"The government, FEMA, the military and the police, they are all in the same boat as we are. They may have contingencies in place, but if this is as widespread as I think it is, they will have their hands full with their own people and anyone within one hundred miles, never mind anyone outside that radius." Harry pulled the truck over and watched a group of men standing outside of a convenience store. The doors had been closed and chained. He wondered if they were going to break through the glass. "Not only that. We are talking about hundreds of millions of people. I don't care what the government thinks it can do; with that many people, they will be overwhelmed and essentially ineffective. Here, in a small town in the Appalachian Mountains, we are essentially cut off from the rest of the world," Harry said softly. He knew he was giving Marilyn a lot of terrifying information, but he wouldn't lie to her; she deserved the truth.

"How are we going to survive? How will I feed and protect Monroe?" Marilyn asked, her hand covering her mouth as she tried to hold back the sobs and horror.

"Marilyn, you don't have to worry. You are staying with us. I will protect you and Monroe, and we have plenty of food in the basement. Peapot's girlfriends have been bringing him jarred food for the last five years. Peapot had me buy a lot of rice, oats, flour and so on, and of course, the garden is doing well. It will be tight, but we will be fine. The biggest thing is security. Earl and his friend will be coming; they will help us keep whole and safe."

"Earl? You can trust him?" Marilyn asked, her voice rose slightly.

"Earl is rough around the edges and he's had a hard life, but he's a good man. He'll do what is necessary, and we are going to need the help. I can't do it all myself, and with two more men, you and Willy, I think we should be able to protect ourselves. Like I said, it is just starting, and it's only going to get worse."

The rest of the ride back to the farmhouse was silent, and Harry looked out the window. It was getting late and people were clogging the roads. Some lifted hands, trying to wave him down. He sped up and many jumped out of the way. They were almost home. He was glad they'd left town and the majority of the population; it was starting to get disorderly.

Pulling up the hill to the house, he saw Earl's truck parked near the house. It was more rust than anything else, and may have been blue at some point in time. Willene came out to the porch and Earl followed behind. Earl met him and stuck out a hand, and Harry took it, shaking it firmly. Earl nodded seriously and turned and went back into the house.

"How is Peapot?" Harry asked.

"He's been fed and is sound asleep. I've got to get in, got lots on the stove. Get cleaned up, you've not eaten and there is a lot to eat, knothead," Willene ordered, her voice sounding like a drill sergeant's bark.

Harry laughed and kissed her head. He turned and went back to the truck to bring in Marilyn's things. The once near-empty house was going to be filled with people again. Harry knew that life as he knew it was over. It was going to be hard, and the others had no idea how hard. He thought about Afghanistan. It was a war zone there, and now it was going to be a war zone here at home.

As he took more items into the house and up the stairs to Marilyn and Monroe's new room, his thoughts drifted to Fran, his Fran. He could feel the ache deep within him, an inner rage at being caught on this side of the world, but he knew his sister and grandfather needed him.

He now held Marilyn's and Monroe's lives in his hands as well. He hoped that it was only the United States that had been affected and that other countries would soon come and lend a hand, but he wasn't holding his breath.

These people whom he invited to his home, he knew he may well have saved their lives, but in having them help defend this house, they could end up getting killed. Every home was a target now, a possible goldmine of food and supplies. If the occupants of a home didn't have weapons, there was no way for them to defend what they had. Many people would be victims, and there was going to be a hell of a lot of bloodshed soon. It was only a matter of time before desperate people came to their home. The mountains were a great deterrent, but desperate people would do anything and everything to get their hands on what they had here.

He brought the bags of food from Marilyn's home into the kitchen. Marilyn was there helping Willene canning meats. He set the bags on the counter and headed back out. He saw Monroe carrying his toys upstairs and the boy grinned at Harry. Harry patted the boy's head and went back out to the truck. It was going to be a lively household for sure.

The young man, Boggy, joined Harry and helped him bring the rest of Marilyn's belongings into the house. Earl had gone to the kitchen to help the women. With many hands, Marilyn's belongings were soon put away. It was getting dark outside and the activity was finally slowing down.

Ж

Mayor Rupert J. Audrey sat back in his large leather chair, his small feet propped up on the large desk. His hands were laced together and resting on his expansive gut while he stared into space. He was trying to wrap his head around the loss of power, the loss of everything. At first, he'd thought perhaps some dolt had hit a powerline, but then that bossy black bitch of a secretary of his, Mary Lou Jaspers, had come in ranting about her smart phone not working.

He'd tried to fire Mary Lou when he took office three years ago, but she'd threatened to go to the NAACP and sue him for wrongful termination. He'd been saddled with her, and it sat in his gut like a rotten piece of meat. His comrades at the local chapter of the Ku Klux Klan dug at him like a rooster on a hen about it. A slow smile creased his florid face. The world had come to an end. As far as he knew, there was no longer a government, no law, no prosecutions, and no rules.

Rupert didn't know if North Korea had bombed them, nor did he know if it were local or countrywide, or even worldwide. His mind raced with the implications. Here he was, the only government, the only power within miles and miles. Lexington might as well be a million miles away. In that big a city, all hell was going to be breaking loose. He chuckled to himself. Here was their chance, he and his cronies from the KKK. The klavern could take charge and purge his town of the unwanted, the blacks, the Asians, the gays, and the Jews. Anyone who wasn't white, pure white, and Christian. There was no one to stop them.

There was a loud knock at his door and it jolted him from his thoughts so hard his feet fell off the desk and he fell, nearly hitting his head on the edge of the desk.

"In!" he roared, shaken by the near miss.

Mary Lou came into the spacious room, her eyes frantic. "Mr. Audrey, I need to go home. I need to be with my family. My car don't work, what am I going to do?" she gripped her handbag to her chest.

"Well… well…I guess y'all will just have ta walk your fat black ass home." Rupert laughed, scooting his chair back up and propping his feet back onto the desk.

"What did you say to me?" Mary Lou asked incredulously, her eyes narrowing on him.

"I said, 'Y'all kin just walk your fat black ass home.' You is fired." He laughed into her angry face.

"You can't fire me, and what the hell is wrong with you, talking to me like that?" Mary Lou's voice raised an octave, her hands curling into fists, her body leaning forward.

"I don't think you understand what has happened, Mary Lou. The world has ended. I'm in charge here, and me and my friends are going to rid this town of no-good people like you, the gays, Jews and anyone else that ain't white. And we gonna get rid of negro lovers, gay lovers, and non-Christian lovers. It is time for a good old-fashioned purge." Rupert laughed in near hysteria when he saw fear enter the bossy woman's dark eyes. "Go home woman, gather your family and get the hell outta my town, cause me an' my friends ain't gonna spare anyone, man, woman, or young'un." He grinned evilly.

He laughed harder as the frightened woman ran out of the office. He got up and put his gray jacket on, smoothed down the wrinkles of his white shirt and left the office whistling. He walked down the street toward the police station, breathing a little hard. He wasn't used to walking so fast, so slowed down as he approached the building.

He nodded his head to the citizens—the white ones; others he ignored. He skipped up the stairs and into the station, his cheeks rosy with joy and exertion. He paused to catch his breath before going to the sheriff's office.

He walked in, there weren't many officers around. His eyes narrowed at Officer Howard Deets, a slender black man with a pencil mustache. He looked away and went over to Sheriff Danny Yates's office. He gave a preemptive knock and walked in.

Sheriff Danny Yates looked up and smiled, curious. Mayor Audrey was looking very happy for some reason. It had started out a good day, and then the damn power went out. He'd had to open the window to let a breeze in. He felt the sweat trickling down the back of his shirt and down the crack of his ass. He mopped the sweat from his forehead with a bright blue bandana.

"What's the special occasion, Rupert?" Yates asked, leaning back in his chair and scratching his crotch.

"Our time has come, Danny, our time has come!" Audrey crowed, a wide grin on his florid face.

"Do tell?" Yates asked, quirking an eyebrow.

"This power outage is our beginning. This ain't no regular power outage, son, this is a miracle. It is an EMP," Rupert laughed.

"A what? An EMP? What the hell is that?" Yates asked, confused at Rupert's behavior.

"An EMP is an electromagnet pulse, that kills everythang electrical, you know, phones, TVs, most new cars, you know, everything. I seen it on a National Geographic program. It's caused by either the sun exploding or something or a bomb, a nuclear bomb. I 'spect that the chinks from North Ko-Rea dropped some bombs and killed our power. Boy, we ain't comin' back from this. There ain't no government except me, an' you of course, and ain't no military. We

48

is in the mountains boy, and we, as in we the Klan, can now control our destiny. We'll run out or kill every black, Mex, Jew, gay or any non-white or non-Christian." Rupert laughed.

Yates sat back in his chair, shaking his head. Both he and Rupert were high officials in the local chapter of the KKK, and the thought of getting rid of all undesirables in their town was just too good to be true. Not only that, they could begin their own chapter, hand-pick their own members.

"You know, Glasglow, Olive Hill, and Shelbyville have the largest klaverns, and we are separated from our own. So, we can make our own klavern, maybe call it New World Knights." Yates grinned broadly, silver shining from the back of his teeth. "I'm sure we can recruit a lot of nice white folks."

"Surely can. We'll be high on the hog, it's pert near perfect. We'll purge all these peckerwoods out of this town."

"Are you saying we should just kill these folks? People won't stand for that," Yates said, shaking his head and scratching the thatch of faded red hair.

"They will leave gladly if we make a few examples. Look, we kill a few undesirables, then post notices for all non-whites to leave. Tell them if they don't leave, they will be executed lickity split. Then we take all their food, an' anything that's useful," the mayor explained. "Now, some things need to happen. First, you need to send your most trusted men to cover the grocery stores, make sure no looters take what is ours. I suggest you kill that boy in there, we don't need no black cops. You need to get rid of him and that big boy, Patterson."

Yates sat back and looked at the mayor. It was an audacious move, and the more he thought about it, the better he liked it. He was tired of all the politically-correct bullshit he had to put up with and walking on eggshells around the two black officers, having to watch what he said around them. To have their world white again, to be top dog, and never look at another non-white face again... His grandchildren could live in a white world, the right world. Perfection.

"You're right, Rupert, this is *our* time. Let's get this started," Yates said, standing up and pulling out his service revolver. He checked his weapon and then he walked to the door, his heart pounding and his adrenaline pumping through his veins. He'd wanted to do this for a very, very long time.

He couldn't believe he was doing this, and his hands shook with excitement. His daddy had told him about a few blacks he'd killed and his granddaddy had killed. A smile spread across his broad features, his face flushed with excitement.

He walked out into the squad room. several officers were standing around, shooting the shit.

Yates walked over to Officer Deets. Deets was looking down at some paperwork when the sheriff walked up to him. He looked up, and jerked back when Yates brought his gun up and blew his brains out all over his desk. The other four officers drew their weapons, crouching and looking around for the threat.

Dimmesdale, the janitor, dropped to the ground and crawled under a desk.

CHAPTER FIVE

"Men, put your weapons away. Mayor Audrey and I are taking over this town. An EMP, an electromagnetic pulse, has taken down our country. What that means is there will be no more power, no more phones, no more cars, unless we got older trucks and cars," Sheriff Yates announced, looking around at the men. "The government ain't going to help us, nor is the military. We are too cut off here in these here mountains. We are now on our own, and we and the KKK will take this town and make it right, make it white!" Yates bellowed, looking around the room again, making eye contact with each of his men.

He smiled with a broad grin, his silver and gold capped molars showing. His already red and freckled face grew redder, and his eyes were nearly wild.

"Sir, this is wrong, this is madness. We can't kill our own, and we can't allow the KKK to put its tentacles into this town. You just murdered a good man!" Officer Stroh cried, his face flushed scarlet and his blue eyes tearing up. He had not put down his gun.

"Stroh, you're a good man and I hate to lose you, but you're fired. Get you and your family out of this town. You have twenty-four hours. If you don't, son, I will kill you and your family," Sheriff Yates said calmly, his blue eyes flat.

Officer Stroh looked at the sheriff, then to the mayor, and then to the other officers, his body shaking violently. He was shaking his head, tears now streaming freely down his face. His mouth was open and trembling, his breath coming out harshly. The gun in his hand, which was shaking violently, was still pointed at Sheriff Yates.

Sheriff Yates walked over and gently removed the service revolver from the young man's hand. Turning, he walked to Officer Gene Grady and handed the man the weapon. "Grady, are you willing to stay on?" At the man's nod, he continued. "Go find ten or more like-minded men and women and bring them here. Me and the mayor will deputize them. I will write up some flyers for all non-white and non-Christian citizens to vacate Beattyville now."

"Yes sir." Grady grinned, and looked over to Stroh. He shook his head. He tucked the extra gun in the back of his trousers and left the office. Dimmesdale crawled out from under the desk and stood, looking in horror at the dead officer.

"I ain't cleanin that mess up. I quit!" Jimmy Dimmesdale cried and ran out, slamming the door behind him.

"Well, shit," Yates said, looking down at the dead officer, the blood pooling on the floor, spreading out.

"Don't worry 'bout it Danny, I'll help you clean up this mess," Audrey said, his mood jovial.

"Now boys, we need to move fast. I need you two to go to all the stores and lock them down. We need to control everything from water, to gas, to food. The same goes for you, Tom and Vern. I need you to find good upstanding folks and we will deputize them. Have them come here, and then we will have them guard the buildings and get this town protected. Go to Deets' house and get rid of his widow, take all their supplies, then burn the house down.

He watched the two officers look at each other, then looked at the dead officer. "Boys, trust me, this is *our* time. Life is gonna get hard. There ain't gonna be enough food for all of us, but if we move fast and are ruthless, we will survive this. But the more non-whites we have, the less your children will have." He pushed his point and noticed the turn-around. Mention a man's family and you have them by the balls.

Ж

The air was sweet, the cool breeze coming from the north. The creak of the swing was rhythmic and soothing. Willene and Marilyn pushed gently against the worn planks of the porch. The aromatic drift of pipe tobacco danced on the wind as Harry drew the smoke into his lungs as he sat rocking in the large wooden rocking chair.

Boggy and Earl sat on the far end of the porch, nearly invisible in the dark night. Periodically they lit the night with the tips of their cigarettes. The tree frogs serenaded them from the verdant forest and the lightning bugs blinked through the dark leaves. It was peaceful, yet the group was tense.

The flurry of activity had been frantic, but most of the food had now been processed. He felt as though the air had been knocked out of him, and his body was tired and wired. The pipe helped calm his nerves, and around the house it was peaceful.

Below, in the distance, fires burned, and periodic gunshots echoed around the hills and valleys. Six hours had passed since the EMP, and below the farmhouse hell was breaking loose. He was grateful they were far away from the violence and the town.

Harry cleared his throat, trying to clear his thoughts. He heard the others shift around him and knew they were waiting on him to talk. He gathered his thoughts like putting pebbles in his palm, and looked out into the darkness.

"There will be trouble ahead. Bad trouble. We need to plan and prepare while we have the time. For now, I think folks in the bigger cities will have their hands full with looting and fighting. But soon they will start to move out and spread out like a disease," he said slowly, his deep voice calm.

"When you think things will get back ta normal?" Boggy asked, a soft quaver sneaking out.

"Maybe in about one hundred years, maybe never," Harry said, and he heard a soft sob from the nineteen-year-old. Harry knew that he'd crushed all hope for the young man, but the kid needed to know the truth.

Harry continued in a soft voice, addressing Willene. "Tomorrow, I need you and Marilyn to do an inventory of all foodstuff so we can see what we are working with and how to proceed with meals." He saw the dim nod from Willy.

"I have a Wonderbag; it can be really useful for making meals with no electricity," Marilyn offered.

"What's a Wonderbag?" Willy and Harry asked at the same time.

55

"The original idea came from Africa, I believe, but it is essentially a large bag with insulation inside. You cook what you want for about twenty minutes, say a stew or chili, or whatever, on the stove or over a fire. Then you put your pot inside the large bag and close it up tight. It will continue to cook your food for up to twelve hours. You use less fuel in the long run, and you have a nice meal at the end of the day. I never liked using an electric slow cooker, leaving it plugged in all day. It made me nervous. I used it when I have a heavy workload...had a heavy workload," her voice choked up.

"That's a good idea, as that will save the propane. How much do we have and how long do you think it will last?" Harry asked his sister.

"We have two hundred gallons of propane, I had it filled two weeks ago, knowing you were coming home and also gearing up for canning season. If we are careful and use it sparingly, we can maybe get two years out of it, perhaps three years. If we use the wood portion of the stove in the fall and winter, we can have propane for maybe another year," Willene said.

"Good. Boggy, were you able to get your hands on some explosives?"

"I could only get a half dozen or more of No. 8 caps and six straight dynamites and four straight gelatins," Boggy said.

"Straight?" Harry asked.

"It just means that there ain't any ammonia in the formula," he said, inhaling deeply on his second cigarette.

56

"What is the ammo situation? I have some boxes of 9 mm and I have my Sig Sauer rifle and a few boxes of ammo for that as well. My grandfather has hunting rifles down in the basement gun safe as well as ammo for that, I believe. I'll have to check," Harry said.

"With all these guns, I'll need to speak with Monroe. I can't have him touching them," Marilyn said in a worried voice.

"I can also speak with him. Teach him gun safety," Harry said.

"I brought my deer rifle an' all the ammo I have, I'm afraid ta say, it ain't much, I ain't got nary but a few boxes. I also got a couple boxes for the .38," Earl said.

"I got a couple boxes of 7 mm, 150 grain," Boggy said.

"Okay. We will need to be conservative on weapons use and ammo, unless we can find more. We need to think about setting up early warning trip wires around the house and property. We need to make sure that Monroe stays in the front or back yards, close to the house, and not go into the surrounding forest," Harry said.

"Down at the drive entry has grown over a mite, I was gonna hire someone to bush-hog it, but Peapot said to let it grow over. With the two black walnut trees down there, it is hard to see that there is a driveway. Maybe we can put up more scrub down there," Willene suggested.

"Good idea. Tomorrow I can cut down some saplings and maybe transplant some down there. Make it more difficult to get through. Make a blind, so strangers going by won't see anything, or at least perhaps fool them," Harry said.

"Y'all recon we go have a look see what's goin' on out there tomorrow?" Earl asked.

"I don't think we should. All the stores will be ransacked if they haven't been already. People are going to be crazy, and if they see our vehicle, that is asking for trouble. I don't want to have to kill anyone, especially locals, perhaps people I know," Harry said.

"You'd kill someone? You'd kill someone you know?" Marilyn's voice rose incredulously.

Harry leaned forward, placing his elbows on his knees as he turned his head toward her, though he couldn't see her clearly. "Our world paradigm has shifted, Marilyn. Perhaps not today or tomorrow, but people you've called friends or neighbors will more than likely try to kill you for the food you have." He heard her suck in a breath.

"It won't be because they are bad people, or evil. They will be desperate. Understand, there are no more food deliveries, nothing coming into these mountains. There are no more water treatment plants, so if people are on town water, then they won't have water, or at least clean water. Once the pressure is gone, there will be nothing to pull the water to the taps."

"I know a lotta folks have wells, so they'd be okay," Earl said.

"True, and there are streams and creeks, but they will have to boil it first. Also, there are no more food-processing plants, the supermarkets and the big box

58

stores only have enough supplies for a couple days, and I don't think money is worth anything now," Harry said.

"I'd say them stores ain't gonna have nothin' there now," Boggy put in.

"I'd say if not now, then soon, they will be empty," Willene said.

A staccato of gunfire echoed along the wind. It was far away, but that wouldn't last. Harry drew on his pipe and the small coal began to glow once more. He shifted in his seat and took a sip of lukewarm sweet tea.

It had been a long first day and they'd gotten much accomplished. Marilyn had been shocked at his suggestion that he'd have to kill someone to protect their supplies and home. She just didn't understand the ramifications.

After a few puffs, he said, "What would you do to feed Monroe? What if you had no more food. What would you do?" Harry asked Marilyn.

"I…I don't know. I guess I would try to find food for him," Marilyn said, upset.

"What happens if you have food, but someone comes and wants it? And in you losing that food, Monroe will starve to death? How hard will you fight to keep that food so your son doesn't cry with hunger?" Harry asked, not unkindly.

"I'd do anything," Marilyn whispered.

"Would you kill to save your son? To protect him?" Harry pushed.

"Yes. Yes, 1 would," Marilyn whimpered softly.

"Good, then I will teach you how to use Moses's gun so you can protect both him and yourself. I can guarantee there will be those out there who will do the same. I don't want to sound cruel or unfeeling. But our world has changed."

Harry got up. He was restless. There was so much to be done and it needed to be done quickly. He continued, "We will be lucky to survive without the infrastructures in place. The fact that we are here and pooling our resources may help keep us all alive. But we are limited, very limited, on what we have. We will have to guard it and be very careful," Harry said, hating to burst her bubble of the fragility of human nature.

He'd seen so much evil and desperate poverty in the countries he'd been stationed in. He'd seen people lying dead in the street, starved, people stepping over them like they were trash. Death by starvation in third world countries was prevalent, and would become the norm in the United States.

"Look. We have gone back in time over one hundred years. Everyday things we take for granted, we no longer have. There will be no replacements for flour, sugar, soaps, toothpaste and so on once they are used up. What we have is what we will ever have unless we find more. If we can't make it, grow it or hunt it, we won't have it."

"Let the Lord guide us," Boggy breathed.

"As you know, living here all your life, that back in the old days people didn't travel more than twenty miles. The distance a person could walk in a day or two. Once our gas is gone, we can only go as far as we can walk. Leaving here in the near future is risky, and so if we do, it had better be for a good reason," Harry said.

"So, we are trapped here?" Marilyn asked in a breathless whisper. He wished he could ease her, but everyone needed to know what was coming.

"No, not trapped, but until the world settles out, it is safer here. Many people will die in the coming weeks. Either by starvation, by being killed by someone taking what they have, by disease from unclean water, by undercooked food or badly preserved food. From lack of medical care as well. Again, we've gone back in time. No one is used to it except maybe the old timers," Harry said, exhaling a long breath.

"I think I will head to bed. This is just so much to absorb. Thank you again for letting Monroe and I live here. I don't know what would have happened had we stayed at the apartment," Marilyn said softly. She rose and disappeared into the house.

"Might aught we set up some kinda watch?" Earl asked.

"I would like to say we have a day or two, but I think it would be best if someone were to stay up and keep watch. I'll stay up for a while and wake you up in about four hours or so," Harry told Earl.

"Okay, and I'll get Boggy up an' he can watch 'til morning," Earl said.

"I'm good with that," Boggy said, getting up and stretching.

Earl got up as both men went out to the back of the house. They had started using the outhouse Harry's grandfather built years ago. There had always been an outhouse on the property. The previous one had been old and ramshackle. His grandfather had a deep hole excavated and a two-seater built over it. His grandfather had been the only one who'd used it up until now; neither he nor Willene had wanted to use it.

Now they had no choice, and he and the men went to the woods to urinate and saved the outhouse for more urgent matters. He would have to make up an occupied sign so there were no embarrassing interruptions. Harry knew they could haul water to the bathroom, but with so many people it was a lot of work and also a waste of a precious resource, the well water. The well in the back of the house had been used for over one hundred years; now it would be their primary source of clean drinking water.

CHAPTER SIX

Harry got up and went into the kitchen. There was a single candle lit to illuminate the way. He picked up the pot of coffee and swished it around. It was still warm. He poured a cup and went back out to the porch. Willene was still there.

He sat down beside her on the swing. She placed her hand over his, and jerked when another barrage of gunfire reverberated off the hills.

"I'm glad you're here, Harry. I'm especially glad you weren't in the air when this went down. Do you really believe it will get as bad as you think?" Willene asked.

"Willy, I think it will be worse, so much worse. People will lose their minds. They think the government will help, but in a few days, when no one shows up, all hell is going to break loose. If people don't have food stored away, if they don't have some kind of backup plan, they are going to hunt down those who do," Harry said.

"Christ Almighty, what are we going to do, Harry? How are we going to survive? We have five adults and I don't know how we are going to make it."

"We have an advantage; we have five adults to hunt, raise crops, do chores, and guard the house. It will be tight, but it is early enough to plant more in the garden. We can fortify the house. It will be a challenge, I won't lie, but if we keep our eyes sharp and we are careful, I think we will be okay."

"I hope so. I don't know if I'm ready for the end of the world, Harry. I'm going to bed." She got up and kissed Harry on the forehead.

Harry took a deep breath. It had been a long day, and it was only going to get longer. The song from Kansas, "Dust in the Wind", came to mind. *"Nothing lasts forever but the earth and sky, it slips away and all your money won't another minute buy."*

Life of ease was over.

Marilyn held Monroe in her arms, trying to stifle the sobs that were slamming into her chest. She was overwhelmed and horrified at the future she and her son now faced. Her hand gently glided over the sleeping child's head.

Monroe was her own heart and she loved him more than life itself. He had been a joy since the day he was born. She kissed the curve of his warm soft cheek. A shudder went through her at the thought of being at her apartment through all of this. That fat man who'd tried to stop them, she'd never come across someone as belligerent as that, and he'd called her a nigger. She'd never been called that in her life.

The hair rose on her arms at the thought of more men like him. What they would have done to her and her son? She hugged Monroe tighter, and when the child groaned, she let go, not wanting to wake him.

Blinking her eyes, she wiped the tears away. What would she have done without Willene and Harry? Her body shuddered once more. A small part of her hoped that Harry was wrong, that it was just some kind of glitch.

After all, there'd been no bombs, no explosions. All was normal, except no power or phones. Didn't they have several Army bases in Kentucky? Couldn't *they* help everyone? Why did things have to get bad? Couldn't they keep it under control? They had police. Couldn't the police keep the peace?

There weren't many people in Beattyville, surely it wouldn't get that bad. She hoped Harry was giving her a worst-case scenario, and maybe things wouldn't get as bad as he said. At least she and Monroe were safe.

Marilyn took a deep breath and blew it out softly. She needed to get herself under control for Monroe's sake. She got up quietly from the bed and went to the window, looking out into the night. A cool breeze was blowing through the window, refreshing her.

In the far distance she saw fires, and knew someone's home was burning, well, a home or building. The echoing gunshots had finally subsided.

She wasn't naïve. She knew the world to be in constant turmoil. But something like this should bring people together. They were all they had after all, right? Once more, the fat man who'd stood in their way came to mind. His hatred had been stamped clearly on his face, directed at her for no other reason than the color of her skin.

She looked over to the bed, at her sleeping child, and hugged herself. Harry had asked her what she would do to protect her son. Deep in her heart, she knew she'd do anything and kill anyone who threatened

65

him. She could feel that monster deep inside her, coiling around and around like a snake, ready to strike.

She'd never ever been a violent person; quite the opposite. Willene had always defended her in school against bullies and bigger children. They'd walked arm in arm on the school grounds. A soft smile of remembrance curved her lips.

No, she wasn't a violent person, but when it came to Monroe, she'd happily and gleefully kill anyone who tried to harm him, even if it meant her dying in the process. He was of utmost importance to her life.

She caught a movement from the corner of her eye and saw Harry in the darkness, walking across the yard. He stopped for a few moments and looked through something; it almost looked like binoculars, but she knew it wasn't that. Then he began walking again and disappeared around the house. She knew she was safe, as was her son. Turning away from the window, she crawled back into bed. Soon, she fell asleep.

Boggy laid curled on his side in a tight ball, silent tears rolling off his face. He held his Bible to his chest tightly, like a lifeline. He'd never felt so terrified and overwhelmed, and he couldn't hear God. He tried to keep the sobbing down, as Earl was asleep in the other bed. He and Earl had been given a room with two twin beds, a small dresser and an even smaller closet.

The house was so much nicer than his trailer, which had been left to him by his grandmother. She'd raised him after his mother left with a dental hygienist in Lexington fifteen years ago. He barely remembered his mother. His grandmother had said they were both trash and he wasn't to fret his head over them. He'd never met his father, and his mother wouldn't say who he was. His grandmother raised him and had loved him. She'd ensured his spiritual health by taking him to church.

Boggy wondered if this were end of days, if the world was coming to an end and the Rapture was coming. He'd thought he'd be ready, thought he'd be happy; his granny always was when she spoke of it. But instead, he was petrified. When he'd said his prayers before he lay down, he'd thanked God for delivering him here to these people, though he'd never lived with white folks.

They were kind, and he felt safe under this roof. He'd known Earl nearly all his life and trusted the man. He was profoundly grateful Earl had come to get him. But all the talk about the hell to come was what really frightened him the most. He'd never had much, never really wanted much, but the thought of everything just stopping? He just couldn't comprehend the long-term effects.

He thought back earlier that afternoon, to when Earl had shown up to his trailer. He'd been asleep, as he had the night shift in the mine. Until that moment his world had been safe and predictable. Maybe he was still dreaming. Earl was at his bed; he didn't remember him even knocking on the door. Earl shook him awake.

"Boggy, you gotta get everything you'd wanna keep an' come with me. The shit has done hit the fan brother and I mean splatted it from here ta yonder," Earl said.

"What? What's goin on?" Boggy asked, sleep still muddling his mind, as his hand rubbed over his face, his dark eyes feeling bloodshot. His brain felt as though it were wrapped in cotton balls.

"We done got hit with some kinda EMP. Reckon that means ain't nothing working, not electricity, not water, not your car, nothin'. And it ain't gonna work for a long time neither. Now get to gettin your shit in a poke or suitcase and don't lollygag. I'll get your vittles and whatever else."

It hadn't taken but twenty minutes, Boggy didn't own much. He'd gathered some photos and his hunting rifle and ammunition. Earl had cleared out the refrigerator and freezer, though there wasn't a lot there either.

They'd then gone to the mine, and it was a buzz of activity, people running all over. It looked like the power outage had affected the extraction of miners. It had been easy for him to slip into the supply shed, which was normally locked up, unnoticed. He'd managed to get a few sticks and caps before he heard someone coming and scrambled out of there. He hadn't even been sure what he'd gotten until he and Earl were on their way to Harry's farmhouse.

His head had been on a swivel as he looked around at the stalled vehicles and people milling around. He'd seen a couple men in a shoving match and people gathered around to watch. It was the unreality of it that was beginning to penetrate the denial.

Tonight, while they'd sat on the porch, he'd taken note of how dark it was out there. Darker than he'd ever seen it, and quiet too. Unnervingly so. There was no hum that normally accompanied everyday life. Nothing. Just those gunshots. When Harry was talking, he could feel the fear wiggling inside him. It felt as though it was trying to push through his skin.

He had wanted to throw himself on the ground and roll around screaming. Even now, he kept his hand over his mouth so he wouldn't scream out his fear. He guessed he'd led a sheltered life. He hoped he was up to the task that was heading their way. At least he was among friends; an old friend and some new friends. He didn't have a choice now, regardless.

CHAPTER SEVEN

Clay's feet were killing him, he'd walked seven miles and it was getting dark. He'd seen no other vehicles on the road, which was strange. The silence was making him nervous and apprehensive. From time to time, he heard gunshots echoing in the distance. Brian was walking beside him calmly, his tongue lolling out the side of his mouth.

Clay stopped and looked around and up the hills, which were green and lush, forested in many places. There was the loud buzz of the insects and, now and then, birds calling from hidden branches. He looked at the sky; it was clear, with thin clouds moving west. There wasn't much of a breeze and he could feel sweat trickling down his broad back. His tactical vest was heavy and was holding in the heat. He wiped the sweat from his face with his hand and then dried his hand on his pant leg.

He'd passed several homes and hadn't thought to stop and use their phone. He would need to now, and when he saw a roof up in the trees about one hundred yards ahead and fifty feet up, he started for it. He picked up his pace and hoped someone was at the house. The pair walked up the long drive. Looking around, he noted that the yard was empty and a little overgrown. Coming to the door, he knocked.

Waiting, he listened, but heard nothing. He knocked once more, then heard some shuffling, so stepped back and waited. The door creaked open and Clay looked down to see a wizened old man. He had wispy white hair that looked like it had the shock of its life and stood in every direction, and wore a faded blue bathrobe, threadbare in places. He had a dull off-white t-shirt beneath.

He grinned up at Clay, all gums.

"Good evening, sir, my name is Officer Clay Patterson of the Beattyville police. My vehicle broke down a few miles up the road yonder. Sir, may I use your telephone?"

"Shor'nuf young man, come on in," the old man said, his voice wavering with age.

Clay thanked him and stepped into the house. He turned to Brian and held up a hand for the dog to stay.

"Oh, don't worry, your'un dog kin come in, he is welcome too." The old man gave a gummy grin, his eyes disappearing into tight triangles of good humor.

Clay smiled and patted his leg, and Brian came in. The house smelled old, musty, with undertones of BENGAY ointment. The living room was cluttered with newspapers and old National Geographic magazines. An accumulation of dust and sadness permeated the air in the home; the word lonesome came to mind.

It was dim, and Clay looked around for a telephone. There was a single stubby Christmas candle on the kitchen table and he walked toward it. He scanned the rooms around him. He noted the ceramic knickknacks and figurines. They were a woman's choice, and he wondered where this man's missus was. Most likely passed away.

"The telephone's in there, the kitchen, on the wall," the old man said, lifting his arthritic knobby hand up toward the phone.

"Thank you again, mister??" he prompted.

"Just calls me Pops." Another gummy grin and disappearing eyes.

Clay smiled and picked up the phone; it was dead. He hit the receiver several times, clicking it, hoping to prompt a signal. Nothing.

"Your phone's out, Pops. How long has your electricity been out?" Clay asked the elderly gentleman.

"Been out since this afternoon, I 'spect. Might as be back tomorrow. Say, it's gettin' dark, young man, would you care ta stay the night? Surely undoubtedly, it'll be dark soon. You'll get stove-up out there in the dark night," Pops suggested.

"Pops, that's very kind of you, thank you sir. I would be glad to stay. Brian, my dog, thanks you as well." Clay grinned as he looked at his dog, who was smiling.

Ж

Earl came to relieve Harry near 2 a.m., but Harry wasn't tired. He went upstairs and set up the rifle on its tripod near the window, then pulled up a chair and looked out. His rifle would remain on the tripod for defense from upstairs. He then took out his cleaning kit and began to clean his Glock. Once that was done, he went to the end of the bed and sat, looking out the window into the night beyond. He felt wired and couldn't seem to bring himself down.

The window was open to let a breeze in. The night was pitch black except for a few fires still raging in the distance. The popping sounds of gunfire had stopped. He would go down to the basement in the morning, take stock of all ammo and weapons in the gun safe, and clean them as well if they needed it.

It had been years since he'd been hunting, but he knew his grandfather took good care of all the rifles and guns stored in the safe. There was a lot to do and it was nearly overwhelming. He took in a deep breath. He wondered if Franziska was safe. He hoped she had enough food and a way to get food. Perhaps it was only America that had been hit.

He tried not to think of Fran; it made him melancholy and tore at his heart. There was nothing he could do about it, no way he could help her. He had to let her go and let his love for her go as well. Easier said than done.

His eyes began to fill and the room became blurry. He wiped absently at them. A breath shuddered from him. He hoped once more that she was safe. He lay his long frame on the bed, closed his eyes, and softly said goodbye to her.

Ж

Hobart Holt, or Hobo, sat in the doorway of Earl's trailer. He'd caught Earl on his way out and Earl had seemed in a hurry. He'd come to have a few beers and maybe head out to a bar. His car had broken down about a mile from Earl's and so he'd figured he'd just stop by and relax. Then maybe call a tow truck.

73

Earl had been throwing a bunch of shit into the back of his truck, and when he'd arrived at the trailer, he'd asked him what the hell he was doing.

Earl had mumbled something about relocating. "I gotta new place to go, but I might could be back later to pick up the rest of my junk."

"Well, hell's bells, Earl, I was kinda hopin' we could kick back and' drink a few beers. Alright, I reckon I can wait. You got any shine?"

"Hobo, I ain't got no shine. Place is yours, there is beer in the fridge and I'll be back later." he'd said, and jumped in his truck and sped out of there.

Hobo had been disturbed by Earl's eyes on an unconscious level. There was something, but he couldn't put his finger on it. Then his friend Robby Rob stopped by, and Earl was forgotten. The two opened the beers and sat back to wait for Earl. That had been many hours ago, and many beers and a fifth of Wild Turkey. Robby Rob had brought some crack and they'd smoked it; it was shitty, but it did the trick.

Now it was somewhere in the middle of the night. Earl hadn't come home and Robby Rob had stumbled out of the trailer at some point and was passed out on the ground, lying in vomit. Hobo looked around and listened to the insects calling out from the high grass that was around the trailer.

Though his head was fuddled, Hobo knew something was different. At first, he'd thought that Earl just hadn't paid the electrical bill, but then others around him in the trailer park had gathered and he'd heard snippets of grumbling during the afternoon and evening about the power and their smart phones. He'd pulled his phone out and looked down at it, but the screen was blank. He'd figured it had run out of charge until he remembered later that he'd charged it that morning.

He'd gotten hungry at some point and went rifling through Earl's cupboards, but found nothing. Then he'd remembered the look in Earl's eyes once more, and the fact that the man had been frantically throwing things into the bed of the truck. Why had he taken all the food? Why hadn't he come back, and where the hell did he go? A worm of unease began to wiggle and squirm in his muddled brain. He just wished he could put the pieces together.

Ж

Harry sat with a small warm bowl of mashed potatoes and scrambled eggs in his hand as he spooned a small bit for his grandfather to eat. His grandfather's teeth were sitting in a glass with blue cleaning liquid on the nightstand. He rarely wore them anymore, Willene had said. His grandfather looked even smaller this morning, as though he were shrinking away.

"Just one more bite, Peapot. You need your strength," Harry urged gently, lifting the spoon to his grandfather's mouth.

"You know, your momma said she's real proud of you," the old man said, a gummy smile lighting his face, his faded hazel and brown eyes sparkling in the morning light coming through the window by the bed.

Harry's dark brow raised in query. "She did, did she?" His mother had been dead for over twenty-five years, and his grandfather had raised himself and his twin. He worried that his grandfather was growing more confused.

"Sure did, and she said not to worry about Fran, that she'll be fine." He laughed and took a bite of the mashed potatoes and egg mixture.

The hair stood up all over Harry's body as though he'd been touched by an electric cord. He'd never spoken of Fran to either his grandfather or Willy. He could feel the uncomfortable prickle on his head.

"What do you mean, Peapot?" Harry asked, his mouth dry. He tried to swallow. He placed the spoon in the bowl and looked down at his grandfather, his body now motionless.

"Like I told ya, your momma said that your Franziska will be just fine. Things were supposed to be how they is. I told you it's 'bout time. Everything is quiet now. The sun took care of that," the old man said and laughed softly.

Harry was stunned. He stared at his grandfather, unable to believe his ears. He closed his mouth; it had been hanging open in stunned surprise.

"You're gonna have some hard times ahead. But me an' your momma will watch out for you and your sister," he continued, his wrinkled parchment face twisted into a sweet smile.

"You knew this EMP was going to happen? How?" Harry asked, dumbfounded by the revelation and unsure he believed it. But that mention of his Fran...

"Oh shor-nuf, your momma told me in my dreams. You ever hear of the Carrington Event? The sun did the same thing here. It took everything down. Your momma told me over a year ago, but said it was a secret. Told me I'd better get busy. So, I did." He giggled like a naughty little boy, his eyes crinkling until they disappeared into the folds of his face.

"Get busy doing what?" Harry asked softly, and the quote from Shakespeare's play, Hamlet, ran through his mind: "There are more things in heaven and earth, Horatio, than are dreams of your philosophy." So apparently there was, for nothing in his life had ever prepared him for his grandfather's words.

"Get busy getting' ready. I told you ta look in the cave. I'm sore tuckered out now and I don't want no more to eat," his grandfather reproached him, yawning widely. His eyes were heavy and blinking rapidly.

Harry picked up the napkin that was lying across his knee and cleaned his grandfather's mouth gently. Harry then pulled the covers up around his grandfather's narrow shoulders and left the room quietly, closing the heavy wooden door behind him.

His tread on the floorboards was quiet, as Earl was still asleep. Willy and Marilyn were downstairs in the kitchen, working on an inventory of their food supply. Monroe was with them, eating breakfast. Boggy was on the porch keeping watch and eating breakfast as well.

He strode into the kitchen and Willy looked up, smiling. When she saw his face, her smile disappeared.

"Is Peapot okay?" she asked, setting down the pad and note tablet she'd been writing on.

77

"He's fine, just put him to sleep. He wasn't all that
hungry," he said, and handed her the nearly full bowl.
Willene looked down at the bowl and gave it back to
him, indicating he should eat it. Harry knew there could
be no wasting food now.

"I'll go check on him," Marilyn said. She got up,
walked over to Monroe and kissed the child on his
head, then left the kitchen. Harry walked over to
Monroe and placed his large hand on the child's head
and squeezed, causing Monroe to giggle. Harry
grinned, then grabbed the pot of coffee and poured a
cup. He sat down at the table beside Monroe with his
bowl of mashed potatoes and egg.

"Can I go play wiff Charley?" Monroe asked, his
sweet face shining with anticipation.

Willy walked over and kissed the top of his head.
"Just stay in the front or the back yard. Don't go near
the trees and stay where we can see you," she said as
she wiped the food off his face.

He got down from the chair. "Okay!" he yelled as
he ran from the kitchen and out the front door. They
heard the screen door slam.

"So, what's goin' on?" Willene asked her brother,
his face still a mask of worry. She sat down in
Monroe's empty chair and cradled her coffee cup in her
hand.

"When was the last time you went to the cave?"
Harry asked.

Willene cocked her head to the side, her dark hair
shifting and falling over her shoulder. "I've not been in
that nasty cave for over ten years. Oft times I kept

finding Peapot there when he'd go missing around the house."

She took a sip of her coffee and her dark eyes clouding a bit in memory, "I had to put a stop to it a couple months ago. I found him sitting outside the cave, breathing heavily. I took him to the hospital and that is when I found out he was in congestive heart failure. I've kept him close to home ever since."

"Do you know what he was doing at the cave?" Harry asked, beginning to eat the potatoes and eggs his grandfather had refused. He took a sip of his coffee; he was going to miss coffee when they ran out. He was going to miss a lot of things. He shied away from thoughts of Fran.

"God no. He was all secretive and acted like a kid, giggling when I asked him. Besides, I had a lot of shift work, so he was on his own until two months ago." She reached over and took a bite of his potatoes and eggs and grinned. Willene had always stolen food from his plate, even when they were children.

"And let me tell you, it has been hard as hell keeping him around the house. I had to hire a sitter until he took to his bed two weeks ago," Willene said, a frown puckering her tapered brow.

"Okay. I'm going to go and take a look and see what he's been up to," Harry said, going to the junk drawer, filled with all kinds of odds and ends. He located a small LED flashlight.

"What is going on, Harry? What has he said?"

"He said Mom told him this was coming, and he has been busy," Harry said, and he saw the soft hair raise on his sister's forearm.

"He said what?" Willene whispered, her dark brown eyes widening.

"He said Mom had told him the sun was going to do this and that he should get busy getting ready," Harry's voice came out as a croak, the hair rising on his own arms at the telling.

Willene sat down heavily in the chair and placed her hands flat on the table. Harry watched as her fingers opened and closed over the red-and-white checkered table cloth.

She finally looked up at him, fear and awe on her face. "Go look, Harry," she whispered, her voice trembling.

CHAPTER EIGHT

Harry left the house a few minutes later. As he walked away from the house, he took note of the well, its rock facing solid and sturdy. The well had been hand dug over one hundred years previously. He could not imagine the amount of work it had taken to dig it.

Back then, most everything was done by hand and took many man-hours to complete. He knew also digging the pit for the outhouse had taken a lot of time and been back-breaking work. His grandfather had hired someone to dig the hole and they had used modern machinery, taking a fraction of the time to complete.

He passed the chicken lot; the creatures were out in the chicken yard scratching away. There wasn't any vegetation; they had eaten that long ago. They threw scraps into the yard from time to time, and the hens descended on it like locusts.

He grinned as they ran over to the fence, hoping for a hand out. "Not right now, you fat fluffy hussies. Maybe Willy will bring you something later."

He laughed when they cocked their collective heads, their bead-bright eyes watching him with gluttony; they always acted as though they'd never been fed.

He headed into the woods behind. The property extended well over one hundred acres and had a vast dense forest, several small ponds, and a creek that ran through and down across the road from their home.

There were many hardwoods in the forest, their canopies blotting out the sky as he entered.

There were stands of beech, poplar, walnut, red oak, sweet birch, red maple, and sugar maple. The ground was still damp, and his footfalls quiet on the moist ground. Morning birdsong filled the air. He smelled ozone in the air, more rain was coming.

Three acres had been cleared for the garden and chicken lot. There had been more land cleared once, but over the decades the trees had grown back and encroached on the homestead. His mother had planted a couple of pear trees and three lush peach trees, all of which were loaded with green fruit. He knew his sister would can most of it. He envisioned peach cobbler and smacked his lips for future delights.

The woods around the cave were filled with pines and a few pecan trees, planted long ago by industrious squirrels. He and Willy would climb into the trees and crack the nuts to eat. The squirrels had never been happy with their presence.

That would be something to keep in mind this fall; he and Monroe could come out here with a few buckets and pick up the pecans. They were a good source of protein, and maybe, with the black walnuts, they could make a kind of nut flour. He knew their ancestors had done it, so it would bear looking into. Especially when their own flour ran out.

Harry kept looking around him, stopping and listening. He heard the call of a whippoorwill and the coo of mourning doves. Then the staccato beat of a woodpecker echoed through the woods. It was cool in the dim woods, redolent of earth and green things.

It was still early morning and some of the tree frogs still sang, unwilling to end their courtship. The terrain sloped upwards and Harry slowed his step. He wondered at his grandfather's stamina. It was a wonder that he hadn't died outright of a massive heart attack.

Kentucky was made up of numerous caves, one of the most famous being Mammoth Cave National Park. The hilly, mountainous terrain of Kentucky hid a wealth of yet-to-be-found caves, Harry was sure. He'd even heard about people living in them full time. He wasn't sure he'd want to do that.

His great-great-grandfather had bought the land, and through the years his ancestors had kept the location of the cave secret. It was a fair distance from the house and deep within the woods on the property. There were numerous rock formations jutting out of the land. The whole property was peppered with natural rock formations. Harry was sure there were other caves aplenty on the property, just waiting to be found.

Though he knew where the cave was, it took a bit of time locating the entrance, overgrown as it was with white ash, flowering dogwood, arrowwood viburnum and various other flora. It had been quite a few years since he'd been to the cave. The landscape had changed only a little, but the overgrowth didn't help matters.

He walked slowly around, and then came across an old rusted wagon; his grandfather must have used it. He didn't recognize it. He finally found the entrance, which was invisible until you were a foot away.

He pushed aside the scrub and turned on his flashlight, stepping carefully down onto the flat entryway. He ducked his head, as the opening was narrow and low.

Immediately he could smell the coolness of something prehistoric, of an antediluvian era. It was dark inside and Harry pointed the flashlight to the ground, though he knew the way by heart. He and Willy had played in the cave for years, it had been like having a secret funhouse.

He carefully made his way down a carved stairway his great-great-grandfather had hewn out of the rock, making the passage through the entrance safer and more comfortable. Within four feet, the ceiling of the entry rose and Harry could stand up straight.

He followed the steps deeper, the air cooling around him. The sounds of the outside faded away. It was like stepping back in time; he could no longer hear the buzz of insects nor the chittering of birds.

When he got down to the lower level, roughly twenty feet down, and shone the flashlight around the walls, the sound of his footsteps echoed softly around the cave. The lower walls of the cave had been white-washed years ago, and he remembered he and Willy had also taken to painting the walls. It had helped keep the vaulted rooms from closing in on them, making the rooms light and airy. The air in the cave was dry, neither musty nor dank.

He smiled when his eyes landed on the homemade couch he and Willy had made. His grandfather had offered to help, but they had said no. Their great-

84

grandfather had also built a couch and chairs, all of which were positioned around the room and much nicer than their effort. Now he wished he had let his grandfather help. He laughed at the misshapen mess as he walked over to sit on it. It was lumpy, but comfortable enough.

Willene had made the seating pillows from old couch pillows she'd found at a dump, using new material to cover them. She had sewn them by hand in the dim lamplight, and been so proud of the end result. He had made the frame of the couch, his carpentry talents sadly lacking. He'd used countless nails and screws and it was as sturdy as a rock. He placed his hand lovingly along the back of the couch.

There was a low coffee table along with several straight-backed chairs, all made by his great-grandfather and all with graceful lines; he'd been a master carpenter, a trait that hadn't translated through genetics. Several tables held oil lamps and candelabras, the candles leaning crookedly. A large box of matches sealed inside a plastic bag lay next to an oil lamp.

Harry clambered up from the couch, walked over and lit the lamp, and put his flashlight back in his pocket. Everything looked the same: the magazines that were years out of date were still on the coffee table, most of them National Geographic. There were a few car and racing magazines, and several Seventeen, which Willy had adored. A soft smile of remembrance curved his cheeks.

It had been the best childhood they could have hoped for. He could almost hear the echoes of their laughter. His eyes crinkled at the memories that flooded him. He walked around the large room, touching things, picking them up and putting them back in their places.

He sighed heavily and turned and made his way to the next level. Holding the lamp before him, he navigated the twists and turns. The cave system had many levels and many caves, alcoves, and caverns. Many of the caves were small, and he and his sister had played hide and seek among them all.

Going to the left, he entered a bed chamber. The entrance had been framed with timbers and a curtain hung for privacy. The chamber had been set up with a handmade bed with rope ties along the frame that supported an old feather mattress. There was a patchwork quilt covering it and no dust on it. Surprisingly, the cave was quite clean.

He'd spent many nights sleeping in this room. He went to the small chest of drawers and opened it. He grinned and pulled up an action figure. He gently set it on the top of the chest; it was GI Joe. He must have wanted to go into the Army because of Joe. He laughed at the thought, and the sound echoed in the small room.

There was a small table by the bed on which stood another oil lamp, a small stack of comics, and an old flashlight. Beneath the table was a glass jar of fuel for the lamp. Another large box of matches sat by the lamp, it too encased in plastic. He left the small room and continued on, coming to another room. This had been his mother's room and held a small bed, a night stand with an oil lamp, and a table that held a pitcher and large bowl.

There was also the shelf that had held her clothes and several photographs of himself and Willy. Harry imagined he could still smell his mother in this room; her perfume, White Shoulders, had been her favorite. A small, long forgotten ache rose in his throat. His mother had been gone for most of his life, yet he still remembered her as a loving mother. He couldn't remember her voice, but at least he had photographs to remember her face.

Walking on, he passed his grandfather's chamber and came to Willene's. He stepped into the room and grinned. There were several posters still up: Boy George, Toto, and Cindy Lauper. The stone walls had been painted a splatter of pinks and purples like someone had thrown up Pepto-Bismol.

No wonder she hadn't been here in ten years, he snickered to himself. He knew he'd have to tease her about her room when he got back to the house. He laughed again at the thought of her as a teen.

He went to a tattered basket in the corner and saw ratty-headed Barbie dolls. They looked like pickup sticks, thrown in with no regard. He laughed again. He couldn't believe they'd been goofy children once, carefree and silly.

He walked on, and the floor angled gently down. There were other rooms with beds, but they'd not been used in decades. Other family members had utilized them way back when, but no longer. The rooms had been left as is, and untouched. Faded patchwork quilts were folded neatly at the foot of each bed, and each room was equipped with a chamber pot. Each person was responsible for their own pot.

He made a face and laughed once more; this had been primitive living, and now they were going to be living primitively once more. At some point yesterday, Willene had dug out several old ceramic chamber pots. From the barn, he'd guessed. Each of the bedrooms now sported their own chamber pot. It was easier than running out to the outhouse in the middle of the night, especially once the weather turned cold and nasty.

When he came to the back of the cave he found the largest cavern, which until now had been empty and unused. His jaw fell when he held the light up and saw boxes upon boxes, all neatly stacked. He walked into the large room, bringing the lamp in close to the boxes.

They were neatly labeled in his grandfather's hand. The box in front of him was labeled "Long-burning candles". In smaller writing, he could see that it was five hundred count. *Jesus, five hundred candles?* He thought. The next box had boxed matches, another box was labeled "Lighters". Another box had batteries, and there was also a box that indicated flashlights.

He looked more quickly at the boxes, his eyes darting and moving to each label, unable to believe his eyes. There were yet more boxes stacked along another wall. He read them. Fifty pounds of dried beans, and there were at least twenty-five or better of those boxes. Then he looked at the other boxes. Those were labeled rice, each box containing fifty pounds, and there had to have been more than fifty of those boxes.

88

He rested his hand against a large box, feeling unsteady on his legs. What the hell had his grandfather done? His brain was overloaded with his discovery. He left the room and continued downward along another passage, finding another chamber beyond.

This one was filled with wooden shelving; he knew his grandfather had built those. They now carried cans and cans of vegetables, fruit, freeze-dried meats, shiny bags, mylar, he thought, of pasta, flour, and powdered milk. The cavernous chamber was smaller than the one filled with boxes, but the wooden shelves were filled with foods of every kind.

He shook his head and once more wondered at his grandfather. There was enough food here to last them all year, and more. There was enough to feed each of them. People would kill to get their hands on this treasure.

Tears welled in his eyes and he slid down to sit on the floor. He couldn't imagine how the old man had managed all of this. The money, the time, and the energy, and it had nearly killed him. Rather, it had killed him, as he was now dying of heart failure.

His quiet sobs resonated off the walls around him. He couldn't seem to stop himself. His shoulders shook as he wept; wept for his grandfather, for Fran, and for the loss of their world. It all came crashing down on him. He'd not realized just how much he'd been keeping it all under control so tightly. He'd not allowed himself to grieve, hadn't had a chance to.

He'd been overwhelmed with the responsibility of having so many people living under his roof, of protecting them from what was surely to come their way. They had no way of knowing, but he did. He'd seen it too many times in other countries.

He had been hoping they would have time to prepare, and here his grandfather had done it all, giving them the precious gifts of both time and space. Room to breathe, to adjust to their new world, to grow and hunt for the food they would need. His grandfather had given them a chance to start a new life without the harsh struggle so many would face in the coming weeks and months.

CHAPTER NINE

Getting up from the ground, Harry left the chamber and went back the way he'd come. He backtracked to the living room cave and then went toward the right, down the passageways that wound around. He looked into the other sleeping chambers, which were all neat and simply furnished. Each alcove held personal knickknacks from decades past.

The cave was like a museum of sorts. There were ten sleeping chambers in all, each holding treasures special to someone at some time. He went on and found another cave with various tools and equipment, and what looked like a crank radio. He wondered if it had been hardened. There were stacks of wires, nuts, bolts, duct tape, and other odds and ends.

He moved on to another cave. This one was filled with firewood and twelve two-gallon containers of lamp oil. The firewood was stacked neatly and looked to be nearly two cords. *How the hell had he gotten all of this down here?* He left that cave and moved farther on. Next, he found a cave set up as a kitchen. There was a large table made, he could see, by his grandfather. His grandfather had a certain style, tending to put slight angles at the edges. He also used whitewash on the pieces he built, because it helped lighten up the space, Harry supposed. Harry was more partial to darker stains with hints of red.

Dishes were stacked along a wall on a counter. There were also pots and pans, and an old crockery jar that held tongs, spatulas, whisks, and wooden spoons.

There were also several oil lamps and, in the far corner his grandfather had chiseled out an alcove two feet long and two feet deep. None of this had been here the last time he'd been in the cave system.

Harry noticed that a trickle of water was seeping from the wall. Not much, but it filled the bowl that had been chiseled out at the bottom of the alcove. A natural sink. From there, the water spilled out and ran along the wall and into the cracks of the floor. Stepping forward, Harry dipped his hand into the frigid water and sipped. It was sweet and had a hint of iron but wasn't unpleasant at all. He shook his head in wonder.

He left the kitchen and walked on, going down farther. This was where he and his sister had played the most. There was a pool farther down, Harry estimated it at nearly thirty feet below ground level. It was the deepest part of the cave. It had a soft decline that ended in a dark pool. The water was clear and he could see the bottom, a gentle slide away, when he shone his flashlight into the water.

He and Willy had always swum here in the hottest part of summer. The water was bone-chillingly cold, so they could only swim around for ten minutes before they exited, blue-lipped and laughing. He grinned at the sweet memory, and shivered at the thought of the glacial water.

The water was sweet as well, and Harry lifted the lantern and looked around. Nothing had been done here. He was glad; he hated to imagine if it had been modified and perhaps ruined. He turned and started back up, arriving back at the living room cave. He went past the couch and shimmied behind the wall to another alcove. Though narrow, it went back about fifteen feet.

Here his grandfather had built a compost toilet. It was a high wooden block painted deep blue. It had a toilet seat affixed to the box and inside Harry found a five-gallon bucket. Stacked around the chamber were bags of peat, pine shavings, and a few buckets of wood ash. Bundles of toilet tissue were stacked up nearly to the high ceiling.

On a low shelf he found bags rolled in bundles. He picked up the bundle and read the label on the bags; they were biodegradable six-gallon bags. He looked over into the toilet and saw the five-gallon bucket had one of the bags lining it. He took note of another five-gallon bucket off to the side, ready if needed.

He shook his head in amazement. His grandfather had thought of everything. Should the need arise, they could live quite comfortably here in the cave. He made his way out and placed the oil lamp on the table. He blew out the flame, took his flashlight out, and made his way to the surface. There was a lot to tell Willy.

Willene wandered through the woods toward the cave. Harry had been gone for a while and she wanted to check on him. Marilyn and Monroe were out in the garden, Marilyn showing Monroe how to weed. She'd laughed and said it was never too soon to teach children responsibility and a good work ethic. Willene laughed and agreed.

She and Harry had often been out in the garden with their mother, though they'd hated pulling weeds.

Now she'd give anything to be pulling weeds with her mother. She didn't mind pulling them now, but there always seemed to be other things to take care of. Now, she guessed, they had all the time in the world.

She took a deep breath and blew the memory away. The terrain was starting to rise and she could feel it in her legs. She slowed when she heard something coming toward her, hoping it was Harry. Her hand went absently to her hip, where her weapon was: a Ruger LC9. She had a holster clipped to the waist of her jeans. When she saw her brother, she relaxed, smiled, and raised her hand in greeting. She saw Harry's flash of teeth and waited for him to come to her.

"How did it go, Harry?" she asked as he drew up.

Harry laughed and ran a hand through his hair. "You're not going to believe this, but Peapot has filled that cave to the brim with everything you can think of. Food, supplies, candles, lantern fuel, toilet paper... he has even built a kitchen and a bathroom."

"Are you kiddin' me?" she said, shocked. She'd wondered what the old man had been up to, and oh, how sneaky he was. She could pinch the little devil.

Harry shook his head, his face going serious as he grabbed both her hands in his. "No, I'm not. I'm talking food that will last us for years and years, Willy. If we plan and are careful, with the garden and hunting, we can easily survive this."

Willene shook her head. She just couldn't believe it. "Should we keep it there and hidden?"

"Yes. We should keep it as a fallback in case we are overrun with refugees from the cities. I don't think

94

we will be, but I just don't know how life is going to be, now that there is no law or government."

Willene could hear the worry in his voice, and was so glad their grandfather had done what he'd done. He'd saved their lives. She shook her head in wonder as she bent and picked up a branch, and then stepped over an ant hill. She plucked at the leaves on the branch she held. As though reading her mind, her brother spoke. "He's saved us, you know. He has saved all our lives, or at least given us a chance. We could have made it without it, but it would have been hard. This at least gives us some breathing room." He paused. "I don't think we should tell the others just yet." He pulled the branch from her hands and began to pluck the remaining leaves.

"I agree. Though Boggy and Earl are good people, I just don't know them as well as Marilyn. I will tell her, if you don't mind, in case something happens," Willene decided, snatching the branch back, grinning at him.

"That's fine. We've known Marilyn since we were in grade school. She is a wonderful woman and Monroe is a cutie. It is good to have a little one around. I'm glad she's here, as I really think she and Monroe wouldn't have made it. I honestly don't know what our future is going to be like. I just can't get it out of my mind," he said.

Willene's eyes cut to her brother. His strong face held signs of stress around his mouth and eyes. He had a lot on his shoulders, but she was grateful. "I know this is very selfish, but I'm so glad you are here, Harry.

95

I can't even wrap my head around it all. One moment it all seems normal, then I hear the gunshots in the distance," Willene said, and threw down the naked branch.

"I know. It's the same for me. Things seem normal, like the first couple days I arrived here, then I see Earl or Boggy and for a split second I wonder, *'Why are these people here in my home?'*" Harry laughed, but there was no humor.

Willene reached over and placed her hand on her twin's shoulder and patted it. "It really is a good thing that you are here. There is a great unknown about to happen. I'm really scared, Harry. I have a bad feeling. We are so blessed that Peapot did all this for us, and that we are far away from town and the city. It's like I'm both scared and numb...does that even make sense?"

"It does. I feel like that too. It is so friggen' hard to wrap my head around. Things seem normal one moment and then it hits me," Harry said.

"Well, all we can do is all we can do. I guess just take one day at a time, hope that we aren't hit with a flood of people wanting what we have. Make preparation, work to keep ourselves safe. I don't know what else we can do, Harry," Willene said.

"Yeah, I am glad we have Earl and Boggy. They can help protect us and we can protect them. Monroe can grow up here, safe, with his mother. It's an odd group, but I think if we all work together, I think we'll do fine," Harry said.

"I know I'm being a little paranoid, but do you think we should make bugout bags of clothes and such, in case something bad happens at the farmhouse?" Willene asked.

"I think that is a good idea, and maybe move some of the weapons and some of our clothes and linen to the caves ahead of us, stuff we don't really need. Have it there so if something happens, all we have to do is take a backpack of clothes," Harry said.

"Because we have redundant medical kits, I think it is also a good idea to put one of them in the cave. Anything duplicated, we can maybe move there, just in case," Willene suggested.

"That is a really good idea. Do you think maybe move most of the foodstuff there? Only keep enough food at the house for a month or two? The thought of someone taking everything scares the hell out of me," Harry said.

"Yeah. I hate to say it, but I'd feel better erring on the side of caution. Marilyn and I can make a few trips and take things up there. I can also show her the way."

"Sounds good, and I will help as well. There is a rusted wagon Peapot must have used. Maybe we can break down the fifty-pound bags of rice into smaller portions, then take the rest to the cave."

"Yeah, I don't think we are going to use all of that sugar either in a couple months. Might as well take that, the oats, flour and whatever else we don't need at the moment."

"How are we with the inventory?" Harry asked.

"With the food you just bought, as well as what we have in the cupboards and in the basement and root cellar, we have a hell of a lot of food. Marilyn and I will make up a menu so no food is wasted. We plan to supplement meals with what is starting to ripen from the garden," Willene said. She kicked at a dirt clod, then smoothed the ground with her foot.

"Good. We really don't want any waste. We can no longer afford it. Hopefully with the eggs and game we can hunt, we'll have plenty of protein. We are going to need it for a good calorie intake." He bent over and plucked the stem of a long blade of grass and stuck it in his mouth and chewed the sweet blade.

They arrived back at the garden near the house. She could see Marilyn and Monroe in the garden. She smiled and punched Harry's arm and headed toward Marilyn, "I'll talk to you later Harry, I'm going to help Marilyn with the weeding."

"Okay, I'll go find Earl, work on the blind. See you later Willy."

Earl stood looking out over the valley. The old farmhouse provided a terrific panoramic view. He took a long drag off his cigarette, letting the acrid smoke fill his lungs. He squinted, the lines carving deep in his face, as the smoke rose and stung his eyes. He rubbed at his eyes, trying to clear his vision. A long stream of smoke exited his nostrils as he shifted his weight off the prosthetic leg. His mining career had been cut short, and during his long convalescence his wife had left him. He wondered where she was now.

98

Barbara had said she wasn't the nurturing type, that being around him and his moods was a real downer, so she'd taken most of their possessions and left. That was ten years ago, and he'd been left to rebuild his life. He'd put himself through a trade school and learned how to fix cars via the mining company's dime.

Earl ran his hand through his thinning hair and blew a long breath, trying to rid himself of memories of her. It didn't work, and that long-ago hurt rose in his chest. When he'd been at his most vulnerable, she'd left him. He'd tried to feel hard at her, but it wasn't in his nature.

Since Barbara's departure, life had been lonely, and try as he might, Earl just couldn't seem to meet anyone new. There weren't a lot of new women coming to Beattyville. Now the world had come to an end and the chances of him meeting a good woman were even worse than before.

He laughed silently to himself and guessed an apocalypse wasn't the best time to date. He shifted once more. He finished his cigarette and went to the edge of the porch and, putting the butt into a can that had dirt in it, ground the cigarette out. They didn't need the house burning down because of a stupid accident.

He was going to miss his cigarettes; he didn't have many left. If the apocalypse didn't kill him, maybe lung cancer wouldn't either.

He sighed heavily and figured he'd get started on the road blind. He left the porch and wandered out toward the barn, pausing at the well to drink from the bucket of water that sat on the lip. It was cold and crisp and sweet, and he dipped for another drink.

Lifting up the lid, he peered down into the well; it was dark and deep. He closed the lid again, ensuring the top of the well was covered. He'd make sure to tell Monroe to stay away from the well; he didn't want the boy playing around it and falling in.

Ж

Clay awoke to the bombastic chorus of the enthusiastic birds, and the distant barking and baying of a coon hound. He brought his hand up to his face and rubbed it hard, soft rasping coming from his unshaven face. The couch had been lumpy and smelled of old man farts.

He was too tall to lie comfortably on the couch, so had had to sleep curled on his side. He could feel his bones and muscles screaming at him in protest. He gritted his teeth and sat up. Brian opened one eye and looked at him, then closed it, sighing heavily.

Pops was in the kitchen, the heavy scent of coffee permeating the living room. Clay got up and walked through to the kitchen. An old silver coffee pot sat on the stove, perking away. The old man was also frying up bacon and eggs.

"Have a sit, son, breakfast is almost done," Pops said, pointing the spatula to the kitchen chair.

"Thanks Pops," Clay said, pulling out the chair and sitting down. He took the proffered coffee cup. He added sugar from an old, chipped sugar bowl. The faded mushrooms that decorated the bowl were nearly worn away.

Looking around, he didn't see any creamer, and was sure that if there was anything in the refrigerator, it had long since gone bad. He'd just drink it sweet, and after the first sip, his body began to forgive him for the uncomfortable night.

"Power ain't turn back on. Guess you have ta walk the rest of the way ta town. I got some old sneakers you could wear, they was my grandson's. He ain't come round no more. Went to live in California," Pops said, sliding a plate of eggs and bacon in front of Clay.

"Thanks, Pops, that will help. We're still a long way from town," Clay said, giving Brian a strip of bacon. He pulled a piece of bread from the plate in front of him. His eggs were a little runny, and so he dipped the bread into the egg yolk and took a bite. It was good; he'd not realized just how hungry he was.

Pops sat down beside Clay at the table and clapped his hands and bent his fuzzed gray head. His mouth moved in silent prayer, then he began to eat his eggs. He then poured some of his coffee into a saucer and sipped at it. Clay's own grandfather used to drink his coffee like that. Clay hid a grin behind a forkful of eggs.

The men sat quietly as they ate their breakfast. Clay sipped the coffee and enjoyed the quiet; it was going to be another long day. He knew he needed the calories, so wasn't shy about grabbing another piece of bread. He grinned at Pops, and the old man returned the smile with a gummy grin.

CHAPTER TEN

Walking on toward the barn, Earl scanned the tree line. All was quiet. He could hear squirrels running through the woodland, and the birds calling as they hopped from branch to branch. It was peaceful, and didn't really feel like the end of the world. He had such a pull to go back into town and look around, to confirm to himself that yes, the world had come to a halt.

Walking into the barn, he saw several loose boards leaning against a wall. He located a saw, a hammer, and a can of nails that was sitting on a work bench. There were several empty stalls. He figured they'd held horses or some kind of livestock years ago.

Many properties had barns; he thought there was a dairy farm down the hill a few miles away that had one. This barn had been well maintained. He knew it took a lot of upkeep to keep these old barns standing. There were numerous caved-in barns dotting the mountains. The weather was hard on them. Especially winters with heavy snows.

Gathering up what he needed, he walked down the hill toward the road. Once there, he proceeded to build a barricade frame. Then he took the saw and cut down saplings of all sizes and attached them to the framework. As he worked, he looked up, catching Harry coming toward him. Harry was carrying a shovel.

"Mornin' Harry. Did you get any rest?" Earl asked, pausing to wipe the sweat from his brow with a faded yellow bandana. Harry was tall and well-formed, and seemed strong and confident. Earl wished once more that he'd gone into the army with Harry. He'd probably still have his leg and most of his teeth. The coal mine had taken a lot from him.

"Yeah, though I can't say it was very restful," Harry said, his smile not reflecting in his eyes. "That the blind we spoke about last night?"

"Sure is, an' looks like you're thinking along the same line, to put live saplings an' turf round so there is greenery an' ain't too many dead plants," Earl said.

Harry grinned widely, saluted with the shovel, and walked toward a likely sapling. It took the men several hours. When they were done, both men backed up along the road and looked back at their handiwork.

It wasn't perfect, but under light scrutiny, it would pass. At night, the drive would be completely obscured. It was due to rain later, Earl could smell it. That would help with the newly-planted saplings and clumps of weeds and grasses.

The large black walnut trees, and the apple trees up the hill, obscured the farmhouse. Farther up the road, however, the farmhouse could be seen. There wasn't much they could do about that, but there was no visible access, at least in dim light.

Earl looked at the house and then the road, and back at the blind. "It ain't perfect, but if someone is walkin', they maybe might pass by, in a car a far peace away, not so sure, but if they don't spot an entrance, they maybe might keep goin'."

"That's what I'm hoping for. It also might give us a few minutes to get into place to defend the house," Harry said.

"You sure you don't want ta go into town? We don't know what's goin' on?" Earl asked, feeling the itch to know intensify. He pulled out a cigarette and lit it, letting the nicotine calm his nerves. He didn't know why he wanted to go to town so very badly it was starting to crawl under his skin.

"I can't stop you from going, Earl, nor would I try, but I know people under stress and duress. I think it will be dangerous. If you feel the need to go, then do, but if you aren't back by dark, I'll come looking for you," Harry answered.

"I just gotta know, Harry. I gotta do this," Earl said.

"I understand. I also feel that need, that determination to go in to town to see what is happening. But I know from experience that all hell will be breaking loose as people begin to realize there is no help coming. It may not be as bad as I think, I just don't know. It may take a few more days. Again, I just don't know," Harry said helplessly, shrugging his shoulders.

"I know I shouldn't go, but I feel like my hair is crawlin' like I got ants crawlin' in it," Earl said, his shoulder shrugging up to his ears. He could feel his face burning red, the heat of it crept up his chest and onto his cheeks and ears.

Harry reached over and patted Earl on the back. Earl looked over and grinned. He shrugged again and laughed. Together, the men walked back up to the house and watched as Monroe and Charley played up ahead of them. The sun was up high and had burned off the early morning haze, but the smell of rain was heavy in the air. In the far distance, gray clouds were gathering.

"It's peaceful here, Harry. Are you sure you want all of us here underfoot?" Earl asked, his gray eyes troubled.

"Earl, I would never have invited you here if I'd not wanted you here. You're a good man, and we will need all the good people here, watching each other's backs. We also need good hunters, and you and Boggy are good men with rifles and, from what I hear, good shots. We'll need that when people start heading our way," Harry said, slapping Earl on the back.

"I'll be as much help as I can. I ain't want to be a burden an' Boggy neither. I'll make sure you and your sister won't never regret it," Earl assured him.

"We have the high ground. Just hoping we can hold it. I think if we can fortify this place, it will go a long way to keeping us protected. That and constant vigil," Harry said.

"I expect we keep on our toes; we'll be right as rain. I'm gonna skedaddle out to town," Earl said.

"Okay, just keep on your toes, and if you aren't back by dark, I'll come looking," Harry said and headed into the house.

The LED headlamp wavered in the dark recesses of the basement. Harry looked around the cluttered shelves, seeing things from his childhood, and smiled. His grandfather threw out nothing, it seemed. He took note of the shelves with jars and jars of preserved foods of all kinds. Stepping closer, he picked up a quart and dusted off the label, which said the contents were cubed beef. Placing it back, he picked up another, smaller, jar. The contents were white and he read "Shortening" on the label. He replaced the small jar back to the shelf.

Turning, he saw several large boxes stacked neatly to one side. Going over, he opened the top one and saw packages of toilet paper. Harry shook his head. His grandfather had thought of everything. Other boxes were scattered around the large basement, many dusty and untouched for what seemed like years.

One shelf held large cans of coffee, and the grin on his face spread to his eyes. Coffee, the elixir of life. They'd have to meter this stuff out carefully, but at least they had it. *Thank you so much, Peapot,* he thought once more. He had a feeling he was going to be thanking his grandfather over and over in the weeks and months ahead of them. This was more than he could have ever hoped for and smiled, thinking of Peapot, giggling while he did all this.

Walking around other boxes and what-nots, he went to the gun safe. Adjusting the headlamp, he bent at the waist and dialed in the combination. The gears moved smoothly for such an old safe. He opened the large door and looked at the armament within. Neatly stacked inside was a Remington AR-15 along with numerous boxes of appropriate ammo, .223 shells, his grandfather's Marlin, and a couple new rifles: an M48

Patriot and Weatherby Vanguard. There were handguns on pegs: a Beretta M9, a Sig Sauer MK25, and a Springfield XD. He laughed out loud. They were certainly well armed.

Along with the weapons were boxes and boxes of ammunition for each one. He was glad their grandfather had chosen weapons Willy would be able to use. He was sure she'd like the AR-15. The scent of gun oil filled his nostrils, and he knew his grandfather had kept all the weapons in prime condition.

He looked around under the long counter beside the gun safe and saw several crates labeled ammo. So there was even more. They wouldn't have to worry about running out of ammo any time soon. Once more he marveled at his grandfather's forethought.

They couldn't afford to waste the ammo, but it should last them. He'd move some of this to the cave. Having all this in the house, and in one location, was dangerous. He would put the bulk away from the house. Perhaps hide some in the barn for ready access.

He thought about what his grandfather had said about his mother. Once more the goosebumps rose on his arms. Had his grandfather merely been delusional? But he had known about Franziska, and Harry knew he had spoken of her to no one. And could it have been a coronal event that had caused the EMP? If so, there was no need to worry about nuclear fallout except for the areas around nuclear power plants.

He began up the stairs into the house, thoughts circling in his mind. Closing the door to the basement, he heard Willene in the kitchen; it sounded as though she were crying. He walked in and saw both Willy and Marilyn holding hands, weeping. Alarm rang in his head like an old fashion fire bell.

"What's the matter?"

Both women looked at him.

"Peapot's gone," Willene said, softly weeping. "He passed away some time this morning. I thought he was napping, and when I went in to check on him, he was gone."

Harry's legs gave out and he sat heavily in a chair, his eyes tearing up. Willy and Marilyn began to blur in front of him. Willy got up and Harry pulled her into his arms to hold her shaking form. He tried to clear the tears from his throat.

"He lived a damn good life Willy, and he prepared us for this nightmare," he said, his voice thick with emotion.

"I know, and he was so happy this morning, I think he knew he was about to go," Willene said, wiping the tears from her eyes.

"Yeah. I heard him talking to himself and laughing when I went past his room this morning. I'm not sure who he was talking to, but he was happy," Harry said, a soft smile pulling at his lips.

"When I tried to feed him this morning, he said he wasn't hungry. He laughed and joked with me," Marilyn said.

"I'll go up and say my goodbyes, and then I'll go up to the back near the woods and start a grave," Harry said, giving his sister a quick squeeze before leaving the kitchen. His legs felt like lead as he mounted the stairs. He could feel the pieces of his heart breaking. His grandfather had been his world for as long as he could remember.

Stepping into the room, his gaze went to the bed. Tears began to slide down his stubbled cheeks. He swiped at them as he walked over to the bed. Sitting on the edge of the bed, Harry took his grandfather's hand in his. It seemed so very small and fragile.

His grandfather looked peaceful, the small smile creasing the old wrinkled face. Harry leaned over and kissed his grandfather on his fuzzy head.

"God bless you, Peapot. Thank you for all you've done for Willy and me. Thank you for loving us and raising us. Thank you for saving us from this disaster, I don't know how we would have faced it without you." He smoothed back the sparse hair on his grandfather's head.

"Thank you, Peapot, for teaching me how to be a man. I can't remember if I ever thanked you. I should have. Sorry if I didn't. Give mom my love when you see her."

Harry got up from the bed and went to the window. He looked out over to the far mountains. The clouds were moving slowly toward them. Several hawks were flying in the sky, and he smiled. His ancestors thought that hawks were messengers to the spirit world. Maybe they were warning them that his grandfather was coming.

Harry grinned at the thought; his grandfather had always been a lively and mischievous man. Willy took after him. He was sure his grandfather would remain so in the next life.

CHAPTER ELEVEN

Earl slowly drove around stalled vehicles, his truck rattling and squealing as it climbed the hills around town, making his way toward his trailer. Familiar faces stood on corners, watching him. The hair all over his body rose. Each of them had the deer in the headlights look, their mouths hanging open as they stared at him.

It was peculiar. Why, after only one day, would they be acting like this? It was like they didn't know what a truck was, or what to do with themselves. They stood in clusters, nudging at each other and pointing at him.

He drove a little faster, looking away. He passed by the Lazy J bar; men stood around outside the door, drinking beer. It was early, yet they looked as though they'd been drinking all night. One raised his beer in salute to Earl and nodded. Earl returned the nod and continued on down the street.

Several shop windows had been broken and shattered. One small grocery store had two men with shotguns guarding it. He noted that no one walked near them, crossing the street instead. He couldn't blame them; those boys looked mean.

Garbage, plastic shopping bags, blew in the once-pristine streets. It has only been a day, for Christ's sakes, he told himself again. Sweat popped out on his forehead, he could feel the uncomfortable prickling under his armpits and he noticed his hands shaking slightly. He smelled the sour stench of fear on himself in the small cab of the truck. He bit down on his lower

111

lip, trying to stop the quivering that was starting from his gut and ending up in his face.

Down a side street, two men were beating the hell out of another man, a bag of canned food scattered all over the ground near them. He slowed his truck and watched, mesmerized and horrified. Harry had been right; hell was breaking loose. He was fairly sure these men had food at home, yet chose to beat the hell out of a guy just for some more.

The downed man stopped moving, and the other two scrambled to pick up the food and stuff it into a poke. They looked up at Earl, froze for a moment, and then went back to gathering up the cans. They didn't give a damn that they'd been caught.

The hair once more rose on Earl's arm. He knew he was seeing something very primitive, not just theft or a beating, something deeper, something base. His nascent brain understood perfectly clearly; survival of the fittest.

He jerked himself out of his trance and pulled away, heading toward the trailer park. He blinked rapidly, trying to clear the tears from his eyes. He knew it was brought on by fear. *I should be afraid*, he thought.

He pulled into the trailer park and noticed many people sitting outside their homes. Once more he felt his skin prickle under the gazes he received. He knew these people, yet their stunned faces held a kind of hopelessness, hollowed eyes he'd never seen before. Their blank stares reminded him of sheep, stupid and dull. The air was silent, eerily so. No children played and no dogs barked. No sound of humankind anywhere, just the breeze and the birds, yet these people were right in front of him. He almost felt he was in a movie, these things only happened on TV, it just wasn't real to him. He had the urge to laugh hysterically, and put his hand up over his mouth to stifle the urge.

Pulling up to his trailer, he got out of the truck. His front door was standing open. He looked around him, looking up the road he'd come down and back the other way. No one was around. He stepped into his trailer and didn't see the fist that plowed into his jaw. His legs buckled beneath him and he fell to the dirty floor.

Earl didn't feel pain at first, though he could feel blood fill his mouth and run from his nose. In his peripheral vision, lights and flashes blended with dusty boots a foot away from his face. His thoughts were fuzzy and he couldn't quite comprehend what had just happened.

"Where in the rat's ass hell have you been, Earl?" a man snarled.

Earl shook his head, trying to clear the ringing and pounding within. The pain was starting to knock on his brain, wanting acknowledgment. He spat to his side, losing the accumulating blood and saliva and several teeth.

"Hobo? What the hell's wrong with you? Why are you wuppin on me? You knocked me so hard, I can't see straight," Earl said, touching his jaw gingerly, wincing at the discomfort.

"I'll whoop you like a broke dick dog, you bastard. You said you'd be comin' back. You didn't come back.

You just lighted outta here, and didn't leave no food, asshole," Hobo snarled.

Earl felt the big man's hand grab his shirt and haul him up. Hobo shook Earl like a ragdoll. Earl's head rocked back and forth, and Hobo's face blurred in front of him. On the periphery he saw Robby Rob sitting on his couch. He tried to grab at Hobo's hands to stop the abuse.

"Confound it Hobo, what the hell? Stop it, damnit all. I clean forgot to come back," Earl yelled.

Hobo let go of Earl and he stumbled back, catching himself on the table. His elbow hit just right on the funny bone and the numbing pain shot up his arm. He looked around his trailer and found it had been torn apart. "What the hell have y'all done to my home?"

"We was lookin' for some grub," Robby Rob said, lifting his hip and ripping out a loud fart.

Earl looked at both men and knew they were coming off the meth: they had the same crazy look as when they'd stagger out of a bar or a party. They had hung together when his wife had left him years before and had been a help to him in recovering. They'd bolstered his flagging ego and had let him cry in his beer.

Both men had started up on meth since then, however, and that was a road Earl would not go down. The eyes of his friends were pinpoints, and he knew when they came off their high; they were mean, like mean drunks. He wished he'd listened to Harry and stayed at the farmhouse. Something in his gut told him this wasn't going to end well for him. Once more the need to laugh hysterically overwhelmed him. He thought perhaps he was losing his mind. His mind began to race, and he began to slowly back out of his house.

"I was a comin' back but couldn't. Honest, guys," Earl said, trying to placate them, his hands up in front of him as though trying to ward them off. He'd never seen them like this, or if he had, he'd been drunk and had not noticed their bizarre behavior.

"Well, we was hungry an' we wants some vittles. You got any in that truck?" Hobo barked.

"What? No. I left beers an' some booze here," Earl said, his jaw throbbing, matching the beat of his heart. He turned his head and spat outside the open door. He'd finally reached it, and was about to turn and run to his truck.

Hobo grabbed the front of his shirt and the big man shook him. "Well, I'm a takin' your truck and I'm gonna find me some food," Hobo laughed.

Earl started to protest and Hobo threw a hard punch into his gut. All the air went out of him and the dark began to swirl around him. He fell out of the door to his trailer and onto the ground.

He made it up on his hands and knees and retched violently. His arms were trembling and he tried to pull himself to the truck. There were people near him, but they were blurry. He felt a searing pain in his ribs and once more the air went out of him and he fell face first into the dirt.

Earl couldn't breathe. It felt as though his ribs had been kicked into his lungs. He gasped desperately, and

once more dark shapes gathered around him. He
noticed that the dirt below his face was turning to
bloody mud. He didn't feel the boot to the head, nor the
next kicks to his ribs.

Ж

It was late afternoon. Harry, Willene, Boggy,
Marilyn, and Monroe stood around the freshly dug
grave. Harry hugged his twin and kissed the top of her
head. Willene had read from the Bible, John 14:1-4, her
voice soft.

*"Let not your hearts be troubled. Believe in God;
believe also in me. In my Father's house are many
rooms. If it were not so, would I have told you that I go
to prepare a place for you? And if I go and prepare a
place for you, I will come again and will take you to
myself, that where I am you may be also. And you know
the way to where I am going,* Amen."

The group repeated "Amen" and began to head
back to the house. The wind was picking up and the
clouds were drawing in, roiling and angry leaden slate
battering rams. It had been brewing all day and it was
finally coming over the mountains. The vibrations of
thunder roiled in the distance, mixing with the faraway
gunshots. The group didn't respond to the gunfire; it
had become commonplace in less than a day. Harry
looked up to the sky, the approaching cumulonimbus
carrying petrichor to sting his nostrils.

Earl had left this morning after they'd finished
building the blind. Harry knew that irresistible itch of
curiosity. He felt it crawling all over him, and for a
moment of madness he'd thought to go with Earl, but

then thought better of it. He thought it was perhaps his many years in the military and the training he received. It was also due to his experiences in this feeling. He knew when to tamp it down and stay put.

He'd said he'd wait until dark, but something told him he'd better go look for Earl before it got dark. With the rain on the way, he didn't want to be out on the streets in the darkness. When you can't see what's out there, it is hard to anticipate a defense.

Willene sat down at the kitchen table, looking over the tablet that listed their food supplies when he walked in. She looked up and smiled wanly at him. He thought she looked tired. He grabbed the keys to the truck and a cold fried chicken leg.

"Where are you going?" Willene asked, getting up from the table and following him.

"I'm going out to look for Earl. He's been gone most of the day and he said he'd only be out a short while. I want to go look before night and the rain comes," Harry said, taking a bite off the fried chicken.

"It is dangerous out there, Harry. Do you really have to go?" Willene's eyes filled with worry.

"I know, but I can't leave Earl out there. I'd best get to it," Harry said, walking out of the house.

"You got your gun?" Willene asked.

Harry grinned and patted his chest; he was wearing his tactical vest, which held several mags for his Glock. "Always."

"Well, don't stay out long, 'cause you know I'll worry. Don't take any crap from anyone," Willene said.

"Sure will. Is it your turn for watch?" Harry asked.

"Not yet. I'll make dinner and then I'll take the watch," Willene called after him.

"If I'm not back before dark, my NVGs are on the hall table," Harry said as he pulled out, and waved at his sister. Once down at the bottom of the drive, he got out of the truck and moved the barricade, then jumped back in and pulled the truck out. He got back out and replaced the barricade.

Ozone filled the air that came through the open window, the breeze humid, pregnant with the pending rain. The wind ruffled his hair, and Harry knew he'd need a haircut soon. He was used to wearing his hair short, practically the high and tight the Marines sported. Now, however, he'd more than likely let it grow a bit.

Did he have any duty to the Army now? Should he report to Fort Campbell? But the thought of leaving his sister and their guests alone in a world gone to hell was a non-sequitur. He could not leave. He'd been on the verge of retirement, and was, in fact, on terminal leave, essentially out of the Army and on vacation. He'd not see any retirement pay coming his way anytime soon...he laughed at the thought.

Perhaps many from the Army would desert and head home, but the single men and women might stay to protect the country. His stomach flopped, thinking of Fran in Germany, and all the other American service members around the world, separated from their loved ones.

They would never see their loved ones again. They would never know what happened to them, if their loved ones were dead or alive. And even if the military could bring them home, would their families be alive or would they be killed for what was in their cupboards?

He swallowed hard. He felt lucky to have been home when this went down. He'd never really thought about if or when the shit hit the fan. Had assumed there would be some kind of warning or something to let him know something was coming. There hadn't been, except for his grandfather's words. It had been quiet and complete. No fanfare, no bombs; just the world stopping in place.

He drove along Highway 52 toward Beattyville, encountering no other working vehicles along the way. There weren't many dead cars, but he slowed around the curving mountain roads, anticipating blockages around the blind corners. He was careful; he didn't want to damage his truck in an unforgiving world. The road went past infrequent farmsteads and homes. He had an idea where Earl might be.

He passed an old man walking along the road, and the old man raised a hand as he passed by. Harry returned the wave, feeling life was normal, then came to an abandoned car. Vertigo ensued as the two different worlds collided and normal met abnormal.

He slowed down when a dog ran across the road. He watched the dog and considered how they might now be endangered. When people got hungry, cats and dogs were more likely to disappear. He shivered in revulsion. He knew people in many countries with overpopulation and rampant poverty did eat dogs and cats, as anything was up for grabs. Now his country was facing the same challenges.

Pulling into town, he slowed and looked around. Two men stood by a non-functioning stoplight, watched Harry as he approached their location. They stepped off the curb and started toward the middle of the road, their intent clear.

On their faces were ruthless determination and cruelty. He stepped on the accelerator and sped up, aiming for the two men, who, in the typical self-preservation of cowards with too much power, turned and ran to the side of the street. They waved their arms and screamed at him as he passed.

Now wary, he pulled his weapon from the holster and laid it in his lap. He'd keep it ready. He scanned the streets. He came up to the bar he knew Earl frequented. Three men were hanging outside, and Harry slowed down. Picking up his Glock, he held it low, beneath the window.

"Hey boys, y'all seen Earl lately?" Harry called.

Two of the men shook their heads and one pointed down the road. He raised his hand in thanks and sped off, not wanting to linger. Some way down the road, he turned down a residential street. Going up and down the side streets, he saw no children playing in the yards, no women hanging clothes on lines.

Curtains were closed, some windows broken. A few houses had plywood nailed up over windows. Here in town, life was more dangerous; there was nowhere to run, and he was sure there was nowhere to hide.

Turning down another road, he saw the Walmart two blocks away. Even from that distance, he spotted five armed men. It looked like someone had taken over the store; for the good of the town, he hoped, but he doubted it. Those who had the most guns ruled now. He turned onto another road, weaving around more stalled cars.

He finally came to the trailer park. Many of those living in the trailer park were very poor. They'd had nothing, and now they had less than nothing. They'd become the third world now, poorer than the meager among them.

If they thought the government was going to help them and were waiting for it, they were walking dead. If his grandfather was right, the solar coronal event had more than likely killed the planet's infrastructures and crippled the governments, militaries and civilian law enforcers all over the world. No one was getting out of this unscathed, especially those who'd not planned and who didn't have the resources.

Though he was sure many of the U.S. government agencies and players were in place with the continuity of government, as well as some military, the fact was there were over three hundred million Americans without power and little to no food in their homes. It was a disaster in the making.

Many Americans shopped every few days; he knew he did. In Germany, he'd never had more than two- or three-days' worth of food in his house. His heart fluttered; he knew Fran was the same. He was sure she didn't have much food either.

There was no transportation to move supplies across the country, no power to get the fuel to the trucks to transport the supplies. Perhaps the steam trains should be brought out and used? He hoped some government entity would think of it and perhaps get the ball rolling. That would take time, time many people didn't have. Within a week, people would become very desperate.

It might take months to get food to where it needed to go, and Harry was certain that the largest cities would be burning by now, chaos ruling the day. The lawless would see this as an opportunity to run rampant, with murder and rape at the top of their to-do list. He was glad he didn't live in a city.

CHAPTER TWELVE

It was only the second day, but Harry was certain the government, if there was one, was scrambling to figure out what was going on. They may have known already and simply decided not to tell their citizens. After all, what could they do to stop a coronal event? Telling the public would have sent them into a panic. However, it may have given some the chance to stock up, perhaps tipping the scales between life and death. Or it could simply have accelerated the killing and raiding.

Had the government set up FEMA camps ahead of time? Had they staged readily available trailers filled with supplies in anticipation of the EMP? He would more than likely never know. If they had, what a logistical nightmare that would be; he could just imagine all the rioting and hysteria.

They were so isolated in the mountains. He'd listened over the years to his grandfather's stories of the old days. If you couldn't walk the distance, you didn't go unless you were willing to be away from your homestead. The Appalachian people had been a hardy people, and had survived and made do with very little.

He wondered at those now alive and wasn't sure they were as hardy as those who'd inhabited this land a century ago. He doubted it. Did any of them keep up the old ways, the old traditions? Life had become soft, easy. Everyone was guilty of relying on electronics. Most families ate their meals out of boxes instead of making things from scratch. He doubted most kept much food on hand, and if it were in the fridge, that would be going rancid soon.

Harry had seen documentaries about the people of Appalachia. When he'd entered boot camp years ago, his accent had been heavy and he'd been teased. Some had treated him as though he were stupid. It was a misnomer about accents and IQs, yet it still happened. To many of his coworkers, he still had a heavy accent, but here he was somewhat out of place; people knew he was local, but he no longer sounded like them.

As he turned down the road to Earl's trailer, he saw a body lying on the ground in front of the trailer. He sped up and pulled to a halt in front of Earl's body. Taking his weapon out and holding it to the ready, he looked around. Earl was covered with blood, and his clothing was torn and dirty. Harry looked around and saw his neighbors watching. None stepping out to help the downed man. Rage flooded his body and he turned on them, holstering his weapon.

"Could none of you have helped this man, your neighbor? Could you not have at least covered him? Keep the flies and maggots off of him?" Harry shouted, the veins standing out on his neck. He could feel the heat in his face and heard the pounding in his ears. The scent of blood filled the air around him.

He watched as the people backed up and scurried back into their homes. His breaths were coming in harsh pants as he turned and bent down on his knee to look at Earl's body. He placed a gentle hand on the barely recognizable face and jerked back and fell on his butt when Earl moaned.

124

"Earl! Earl, can you hear me?" he nearly shouted. Earl groaned a little louder, and Harry opened the passenger-side door to the truck. He put his hands under Earl's armpits, hoisted the semiconscious man up, and leveraged him into the truck. He swung Earl's upper legs up and into the truck, eliciting a loud cry from Earl.

"Sorry brother, I know it hurts, I'll get you home ASAP," he murmured.

He looked franticly around for Earl's prosthetic leg and saw it lying under the trailer. He ran to the trailer, bent down and pulled the leg out, then threw it onto the floorboard. He slammed the door hard enough to rock the truck. He ran around and climbed into the driver's seat, then peeled out of the trailer park, rock, dirt, and trash flying out behind him.

Harry's hands were gripping the wheel so hard that his knuckles where white and the tendons corded along the bone. Harry looked over to Earl and could see the blood flowing again; he must have opened up the wounds. Bloody bubbles were coming out of the man's mouth as he breathed.

Harry flew down the residential streets, the truck fishtailing along the turns and curves of the roads. Once on the straightaway, he floored it, the wind blowing through the truck's open windows like a storm. The sun was setting and the clouds were gathering in angry consultation, their thunderous voices loud and menacing.

Large drops of water splashed against the windshield and the heavens opened up, letting a rush of precipitation fall in sheets. Harry flipped on the wipers, and streaks blurred his view. Brilliant light flashed across the sky, leaving a negative image in the back of Harry's retinas. He blinked rapidly to clear his eyes.

Harry squinted through the windshield, the rain coming into the truck cab to soak both of them. He bit the inside of his cheek when he had to slow down on hairpin curves. He tried to speed up, only to slow down again to maneuver around the abandoned cars. He hit the steering wheel with the palm of his hand, frustration rising along with his fear.

He had to slow even more due to the hard rain; he didn't want to fishtail off the side of the mountain. He'd also not belted Earl in, and was afraid the man would be knocked around too much.

Soon he was nearly home and began to breathe a little easier. He saw a flash of something and felt a thump on the left front bumper. He hit the brakes and the truck fishtailed, then came to a rocking stop. Harry jumped out and went to see what he'd hit.

A large buck lay on the far side of the road, its hind legs broken. The poor creature continued to struggle up and tried to run, only to fall once more. The animal's dark liquid eyes rolled in panic and its front legs kicked wildly. Harry was sorry the beautiful animal had been hit.

Pulling his Glock, he quickly ended the creature's suffering. Then he grabbed the hind legs and pulled the buck to the back of the truck. Putting down the tailgate, Harry grabbed a coil of rope from the bed of the truck and tied the rope around the deer's legs, running the other end of the rope through a metal loop at the back of the truck bed. He pulled on the rope, hoisting the deer.

His adrenaline still pumping, he pulled hard, grunting with the effort, and guided the deer into the bed of the truck. The copper tang of blood and cordite filled his nostrils. He pushed and pulled and cursed, wanting to get the carcass into the truck as fast as he could.

Once the deer was in the truck, Harry got back into the cab and drove the rest of the way home. He kept wiping the blood from his hands onto his jeans. It was near full on dark now and the rain heavy. He drove up to the barricade, jumped out and moved the structure, then pulled the truck in and replaced the blind.

He drove up to the house, beeping the horn. The truck shimmied and rocked heavily as he came to a stop. The house was dark, but he saw a flashlight heading toward him. It was Willy, and Marilyn was behind her.

"Earl's been hurt. Can you help me?" Harry called. Boggy came from around the side of the house. Everyone helped to ease Earl out of the truck and into the house. They took him into the living room and laid him on the floor. Willene went to the fireplace and retrieved the hurricane lantern from the mantle, then lit it with the box of matches that usually sat by the lantern.

Placing the lantern on the table, Willene turned to Harry. "Go get more lanterns, and put them on the table, let's get this room lit up. Marilyn, in my bedroom closet is an emergency kit. Can you bring it here please?" Willene ordered, the nurse in her taking charge.

Harry hurried back to the living room with two lanterns, lit them, and then went to the coat closet and pulled out another. The room was now bright, and he turned to see Marilyn coming down the stairs with a large duffle bag. She brought it to Willene and knelt down to help.

Both women began to gently cut the clothes away from Earl's body. The man groaned, tears sliding down his bruised and bloodied face. Harry went to the upstairs linen closet and pulled out some old sheets and a quilt. He returned to the living room and gave them to Willene.

"We got this, Harry. Go eat something," Willene ordered her brother.

Boggy and Harry went to the kitchen. There were strips of fried steak and cornbread in a cast iron skillet. Harry went to the sink and dipped water out of the small bucket that sat beside the sink. He poured it over his hands and reached for a bar of soap.

Once clean, he noticed his hands were still shaking. He walked over to the stove. Sitting beside the fried steak and cornbread was a pot of soup beans with a large ham hock. The food was good and filling.

Willene was still using the last of the food from the freezer. They would be tightening their belts soon enough. Thankfully, if they used the food in the cave wisely, harvested crops and hunted meat, or hit them like the deer, they should eat well.

"What happen to Earl? Who done stoved his head in?" Boggy asked, sipping on warm sweet tea, his eyes large and luminous in the candlelight.

"I don't know, but someone nearly beat him to death. Worse, his neighbors didn't even lift a finger to help him," Harry said, his anger coming through in his voice. He could feel the rage beginning to build again and tried to tamp it down.

"I expect they probably still in shock. I S'wanee, them folk is maybe titched in the head, ain't able to think straight," Boggy said.

"Maybe, but still, I can't believe they didn't at least help him a bit, give him water or shade him," Harry said.

"I suspect it's good that it was cloudy, I know that's good for him. He'd like to have died," Boggy replied.

"True, Boggy. I got a deer in the back of the truck, hit it on the way back. Can you help me get it to the barn to hang it? I need to bleed it and then butcher it," Harry said, stifling a belch.

"Dang, you're sure as sugar good, Harry. Saved a man and bagged a deer." Boggy grinned, placing his plate in a pan full of soapy water. He washed his plate and fork, then rinsed them off in the sink with clear water. He placed his dish in the rack to dry. Harry followed suit.

Pulling the truck to the barn, he and Boggy hauled the deer off the back and dragged it into the barn. He left the truck's lights on to illuminate the interior. They hung the deer from its hind legs from a tackle rig on a

129

beam. Harry went back into the house and retrieved a knife. It was sharp; both Willene and Peapot kept the knives sharpened.

Boggy dragged a large galvanized bucket over and placed it under the deer, his dark skin glistening with sweat and mist. Boggy held the head as Harry took the knife and slit the neck on each side. Blood slowly began to empty into the pan. Then Harry carefully made a slit, beginning between the hind legs, and pulled the skin outward: he didn't want to puncture the membrane that held the guts of the deer.

It took some time, but with Boggy's help the deer was soon skinned and the guts neatly removed. Harry then took a five-gallon bucket and walked down to the well and filled it. Bringing it back to the barn, he and Boggy cleaned up the carcass and themselves.

"Why don't you take a peek on Earl," Boggy suggested. "I can finish. I'll take this critter to the root cellar, hang it and let it rest."

"Thanks, Boggy, I appreciate that. Then come on in and we'll see what's what for the rotation watch tonight," Harry said.

Harry walked back to the house. He didn't need a flashlight, knowing the path by heart as he did. He wondered once more what had happened to Earl. They had removed his leg and beaten the man to within an inch of his life. Had Earl walked into some kind of trap, or had these people come through while he was home?

The thought of the neighbors standing around not lifting a hand enraged Harry once more. He sucked in a breath, knowing it was pointless. It certainly wouldn't

130

help Earl if Harry's head exploded from rage. But those people had just stood by and watched a man be beaten nearly to death and hadn't lifted a finger to help. To hell with them all.

The world had always been a violent place, he knew that very well. He'd seen it at many of his duty stations. The violations had been horrific and gave him nightmares. He'd seen fist fights, and been in a few himself, but he'd not seen someone he knew beaten to within an inch of his life.

To know that the people who knew Earl had just stood there and watched, not giving a damn...Harry couldn't wrap his mind around that. Maybe Boggy was right, maybe they were in a state of shock.

It snapped something within him. A dark small voice said it was glad the world had gone to hell, that those assholes would not survive. He was immediately ashamed of himself. He'd not been raised like that, and he knew his grandfather would be ashamed of him.

Angry, he wiped the tears away. He'd not even known he'd been crying, or perhaps it was rain. He was fighting to gain control of himself. The death of his grandfather and near-death of his friend so close together was just too much to take in, not to mention the loss of Fran. He took in a deep breath, held it and blew it out.

He entered the house. It was dark and quiet, but the light in the living room was still on. He grabbed a chunk of cornbread and ate it, then found his coffee. It was cold, but he didn't care. The cornbread was good

and he washed it down; it went well with the cold
coffee. He sighed heavily and felt his nerves settling.

CHAPTER THIRTEEN

Dr. Katherine Lee sat in her office. She'd not been home since the power had gone out and the world as she knew it had ended. So many people needed her help. They'd lost five elderly people and one child that had been on life support. The backup generators had never come on and all equipment had stopped. The hospital was eerily quiet.

She rubbed her face hard, exhaustion settling over her. She'd been going for over twenty-four hours now and saw no end in sight. She worried for her parents, knowing they worried for her. They were second-generation Korean Americans, her grandparents' exiles from North Korea. South Korea hadn't been that welcoming, so her grandparents had emigrated to America. They had ended up in Lexington, Kentucky, where there was a small North Korean community.

Her father had met her mother in Lexington, married, and had helped his parents with their Korean restaurant. When Katherine came along, she was their pride and joy and hope for the future. They saved money for medical school and Katherine thrived and excelled. She and her parents had come to Beattyville, where she'd set up practice. She was a good doctor and her patients loved her.

Katie stepped into a darkened room where a candle was burning. She could make out the patient, a saline bag hanging from the hook next to him. There wasn't much they could do for the patients now except keep them hydrated and sedated. She went over and felt the young man's head; his head was cool. She didn't want to wake him, as he'd been in terrible pain earlier in the day. She left the room and walked up the hall.

She couldn't give up on them now. Dr. Walton Blue had disappeared sometime during the night and no other doctors had come to relieve her. There were a few nurses left, and a couple orderlies. Her friend Willene Banks was on her time off. Would she be able to even make it in?

Willene lived over thirty minutes away and her grandfather was dying. She knew Marilyn had been going over to help in her role as a hospice nurse. She was glad, as Marilyn was a compassionate nurse. They needed more like her.

No, Willene won't be here. She has a lot on her plate, Katie thought. She couldn't blame her. She couldn't blame the others for leaving. Her phone no longer worked, the computers were dead, and the toilets no longer flushed. The rancid stench of sewage was starting to permeate the hospital corridors. The CNAs had left and so had maintenance. Something had to change soon, as keeping the patients clean was getting harder. They had to be careful of disease and infection.

For the one-hundredth time she asked herself what in the hell was she going to do? What was going on? What had happened, and where were the police, or maybe even the military or National Guard? No one had any answers.

For now, it was quiet. She found an empty room and lay down in the bed. It was raining outside, which sounded wonderful. She shifted onto her side and looked out into the dark night, her eyes growing heavy. And then she was asleep.

Ж

Clay's feet were killing him, even with the shoes Pops had given him. He looked up to the sky. The clouds had been threatening all day. He looked down at Brian and bent to pet the dog's head. He looked up and down the road. Deserted, unnervingly silent but for the insects that buzzed in the brush along the road. He'd seen only one vehicle all day, and that had been disabled like his own.

"Brian, where the heck did everybody go?" Clay asked the dog, who tipped his head from side to side. Clay grinned at Brian, then sat down in the middle of the road. Gravel bit into his rear end, so he shifted a bit until he was comfortable. Then he opened his pack and pulled out a bottle of water and Brian's water dish.

Pouring the clear liquid into the dish, he shoved it toward the dog, who began to lap up the water greedily. Clay tipped the bottle and drank heavily. He looked into the gray, angry sky again. He was still another day or two from town. He'd have to look for another home to sleep in. He hoped someone would allow him to.

Pops had been very nice, giving him more water from his hand pump out in the back yard. It had been an ancient thing but pulled the water up readily. The man had also made him several peanut butter and jelly sandwiches on stale bread; they'd finished the other loaf over breakfast.

Clay pulled out one of the sandwiches and began to eat it, thankful for the energy. He'd eaten the beef jerky, which made him thirsty. He'd also eaten the three apples Pops had given him, along with a fruit cup.

The apples had been from the grocery and didn't have the sweetness of those fresh off a tree. He was hungry, though, and had chewed through them, even eating the cores. He was a big man with a big appetite. The extra food had gone a long way in quieting the rumblings. It was too early yet for wayside berries; he'd seen them along the road, plump but green.

He dug around in the pack and pulled out Brian's dry dog food and dumped some into the empty dish. Clay inhaled deeply and rotated his head from side to side, easing the muscles in his neck. He wiped the sweat from his face, glad there was a cool breeze. Some blue jays squabbled loudly in a nearby bush. He squeezed his feet and stretched them, easing the muscles. The sneakers fit okay, but the long day of walking was wearing on him. He looked into the pack and laughed; Pops had also given him a roll of toilet paper.

He groaned as he got up, and he heard his vertebrae pop like soft gunfire. His knees didn't thank him either, popping loudly. "Come on, boy, we need to find a place to lay our heads. Let's hope they are as nice as Pops."

Brian cocked his head and wagged his tail and grinned once more at Clay. Clay laughed and patted the dog's head.

Ж

Harry finished the cornbread and finished wiping the rain and crumbs from his face. Taking a deep breath, he went into the living room. Earl was now on the couch, an old butter soft quilt pulled up around him. The women were out on the porch; he could hear the swing creaking softly.

Harry knelt down beside Earl and looked into the beaten face. It was bad, and he wondered if Earl's bones were shattered. He laid a large hand on Earl's shoulder and felt the man stir under his touch.

"I already know the answer, but how are you feeling?" Harry asked.

"Like hammered dogshit," Earl mumbled, and laughed weakly.

"Do you know who beat you, Earl?" Harry asked, his voice low and calm.

"Yeah, couple friends, or ex-friends. Them peckerwoods was a little high off meth. Wanted food an' my truck. When I ain't have no food, they done beat the tar outta me. I suspect they took my leg and beat me with it," he said and laughed, though no humor was evident.

"Bastards. I got your leg. I don't think they broke it," Harry said, tamping down the anger that threatened to take his breath away.

"I thought I was done for, Harry. Ain't nobody even try to help me. I just lay on that ground, all stove up, gettin' the tar kicked out of me and them neighbors of mine just stood watching," Earl choked, a sob rising from his chest.

"Don't worry about that, Earl. You're safe now among friends," Harry said, laying his hand on the broken man's shoulder. "Get some rest. We got you and we'll keep you safe, brother."

Harry left Earl to heal in his slumber and walked out onto the porch. It was dark and the rain fell heavily now, thundering on the metal roof of the farmhouse. Talking was impossible, so he sat in the rocker near the women and looked out into the valley. It was dark as pitch, and the rain obscured all else.

He took his pipe out of his pocket and lit the tobacco. Inhaling the fragrant smoke, he let it curl and seep in. He could feel the smoke swirling gently in his lungs and held it there a moment or two.

Letting the smoke out, he released the tension. But his thoughts were like pinballs, striking on every side of his brain. There wasn't much that could be done about the men who'd beaten Earl. There was clearly no law, or at least any semblance of law and order.

Earl could take matters into his own hands, and Harry would back him up, but it would take time for Earl to heal. He'd wait and see what the man wanted to do.

The rain slackened after a time and became a light drizzle, the humidity beginning to rise. He drew on his pipe again. Harry looked over to the women, who were still swinging slowly. He could barely make out their forms.

"What was the damage?" Harry asked to no one in particular.

"Well, he's lucky to be alive, that's for sure," Willene answered him. "He has some cracked ribs, and perhaps a fractured radius on his left arm as well as broken fingers. We splinted up the arm and fingers, to keep that side immobile."

"He has numerous contusions and abrasions, and they knocked out a couple teeth. He also bit the hell out of his tongue. That will have to heal on its own. We stitched up the worst of the gashes. We don't know about internal damage, we'll just have to wait and see," Marilyn added.

"Does he know who did this to him?" Willene asked.

"He said it was a couple of friends," Harry said flatly.

"Lord have mercy," Marilyn said.

"What's worse, his neighbors just stood and watched as he was nearly beaten to death," Harry said, his voice rough with suppressed anger.

"I don't understand how people can just stand by and watch someone be hurt like that," Willene said.

"I don't either. Was there not one man among them that would step in?" Marilyn asked.

"No, none. They all stood looking at me as I loaded Earl into the truck. They looked like sheep, their faces stupid and blank," Harry said, taking a long draw on his pipe. He let the smoke go from his nostrils like an angry dragon, the eddies moving outward.

"These people were more than likely like that before the power ended," Willene said.

"Yep. Useless people. Not worth spit," Harry agreed.

They all looked around as Boggy stepped out onto the porch. They could barely make out his silhouette as he crossed the porch and sat in one of the rockers.

"I checked on Earl, he's sleepin'," Boggy said to no one in particular.

"I'll take first watch. I'm too wired up to sleep. I'll get you up, Willene, about 2 a.m. if that is okay?" Harry said.

"What time is it now?" Boggy asked.

"I'd say about nine," Willene said.

"Seems later. I'm headed to bed. It's been a long day," Marilyn said, getting up from the swing.

"There is cornbread and beans on the stove if you're hungry later on, Harry. Good night," Willene said as she too left the porch.

Boggy and Harry sat quietly in the dark. The silence was broken by tree frogs croaking and high chirps that started up a chorus. The rain had all but stopped. Buzzing crickets joined in joyfully, then the cicadas added their humming, drowning out the silence.

"What happened to Earl? I was gonna ask him, but he was sleepin', so I didn't," Boggy said.

"Earl said a couple of meth head friends were at his trailer, and when he didn't have food, they beat him and took his truck," Harry said, relighting his pipe.

"That'd be Hobo and Robby Rob. I've seen them hangin' out 'round his place," Boggy clarified.

"You mean Hobart Holt? And Robert Robinson? They were a grade behind me in high school. What the hell happened to them?" Harry asked, shocked that he knew these men, and at what they'd done to Earl.

"Well, Hobo got stove up in the mines and got hooked on painkillers. When that weren't enough, he hooked up with Robby Rob and they got into meth. They been losers for years, ain't worth nothin' to no one. I ain't surprised they nearly killed Earl. Sorry peckerwoods, the both of 'em," Boggy said, turning and spitting off the porch.

"The world has gone to hell, and all the cockroaches have come out from their hiding places. The bad people will become truly bad and will take advantage of the collapse. By the way, Boggy, what is your given name?" Harry asked, drawing deeply on his pipe.

"Beauregard Hines. Lord baby Jesus help us all. How are we gonna protect ourselves?" Boggy asked.

"The best we can, I expect. We have several things working in our favor, Boggy. First, we are well away from town. Though locals know of the farmhouse, the outsiders won't. Another good thing, we are very far away from Lexington. Hopefully the barricade blind will grow and fill in, to keep us hidden. We have my NVGs for night watches, and I've started putting up early warning traps around the property," Harry said.

Boggy laughed sheepishly. "Yeah, I tripped over a couple, dang near gave me a fright. I'll help tomorrow with setting more."

"I don't think we should leave the property again, any of us. There isn't anything out there that we need. And chances are, if we do leave, someone could follow us back," Harry pointed out.

"I agree Harry, it's scary out there and I ain't even seen it. I know people get crazy at all the after-Thanksgiving sales, I don't even wanna think 'bout starving folks and what they would do," Boggy said.

"I've seen more evil in this world than I care to say. That was in third world countries. We've now become a third world country. There are millions out there with no way to get food to survive except to take it from those who have it. Make no mistake, desperate people will kill for even the smallest amount of food, and it won't take but a few days," Harry said.

"Yeah, the lazy folks, they just keep on being lazy and they're gonna steal from others who worked hard. I seen it all my life. Lots folks has a scratch of land, but they don't even plant a garden," Boggy said.

"Yes, and if groups of evil people band together as they seem to do, we'll be seeing more violence heading our way. I've heard that stores no longer keep large stocks of food, that they bring it in every couple days. I passed Walmart to Earl's place and there were men out front with weapons, guarding it."

"You think they gonna help the hungry folks?" Boggy asked.

"Don't know. I hope so, but chances are, no they won't. They'll keep it for themselves. If that is so, then people are going to be hurting quick. I don't know what the local government has set up as far as an emergency contingency plan," Harry said.

"If they don't know how to hunt, they ain't gonna be able to get meat. Maybe the best time for them ta plant a good garden, but it ain't gonna grow fast. I suspect we got our work cut out for us." Boggy laughed softly, getting up. He walked pass Harry and patted him on the shoulder, then headed into the house.

Harry smiled to himself. Though Boggy was nineteen, he was still a kid and was trying to adapt to the new world and be a man. He was a good kid, though, and Harry liked him. He was a hard worker and an honest young man. Harry was glad the kid was here; they'd need him.

He stood and walked up and down the porch, looking through the NVGs, then went down off the porch and around the house to the back, scanning the tree line with the NVGs. The chorus of critters filled the damp night air, and the smell of ozone permeated everything around him. Dampness surrounded him and his skin captured droplets, which coalesced and dripped down his face.

CHAPTER FOURTEEN

Hobo sat on the dirty ill-sprung couch, littered with old cartons of fast food. The house stank like old farts and mold. His stomach rumbled loudly. He watched as cockroaches skittered freely across the floor, uninhibited by human presence. The cockroaches crawled in and out of scattered empty food containers, their tiny scratching filling the silent room.

Hobo picked his left nostril and flicked something across the room at one of the insects, missing. He wiped his finger on his belly. He looked to the kitchen and saw Robby Rob's body sprawled out, his chest rising and falling in rhythmic slumber. Hobo scratched his hairy belly, lifted his hip, and ripped out a burbling fart.

"Wake up, Robby, I'm hungry. We need ta go find some grub," Hobo bellowed, eliciting a jerk from the prone man. Slowly, Robby Rob sat up, his dark face gray in the dim sunshine that penetrated the heavy drapes. Hobo could hear the scrape of stubble as the sleepy man scratched at his jaw.

Robby Rob slowly rose, a staccato of thunderous farts added to the fug in the apartment. "I thank I shit myself," Robby Rob said, shaking his left leg, jigging something loose. He turned and disappeared into the bathroom.

Hobo struggled from the couch and went to the window, pulling the heavy drapes open. His head jerked back from the stabbing pain of bright light that flooded the room. Dust motes danced in the shafts of

144

light that spilled in, illuminating the filthy floors. The cockroaches scurried for cover, searching for cool darkness and safety.

Once more Hobo scratched his hairy belly. He scanned the road below the second story apartment. He noticed Earl's truck parked half up on the curb, a rubber trashcan pinioned beneath it. Two youths were looking into the truck and he rapped hard on the window, shouting, "Git the hell away from my truck young'uns little shits." He grinned, his discolored and rotted teeth glistening in the light, as he watched the boys scatter.

"The toilet ain't flush, and the dang water don't turn on," Robby Rob complained, coming back into the living room." He wore a different pair of jeans, but Hobo could still smell shit on him.

"Don't you remember, ya idjit? The damned world has come ta an end. Ain't no power and no electricity," Hobo spoke as though to a simpleton.

"Oh yeah, I remember now. I'm hungry, we need ta finds us some food," Robby Rob lamented.

"I was thinkin' the very same thing. Let's go to the QuickMart and see what's for breakfast," Hobo laughed.

Both men left the apartment and made their way to Earl's truck. The truck started up and they pulled off the curb, leaving the rubber trash can behind. The trip only took a few short minutes, winding in and out of abandoned vehicles. They pulled into the QuickMart and noticed the windows had been busted out.

"Shit, looks like someone's beat us to it," Hobo said, frustration lacing his voice.

"Let's look anyway, we might could find some shit," Robby Rob said, opening the passenger's door before the truck came to a stop.

Going in, Hobo saw an old man digging through a pile of debris knocked over from the shelves. The old man ignored the newcomers, continuing to comb through papers and boxes. Hobo walked over and kicked the old man hard. "Get the hell outta here old man, this is mine," he barked.

The old man staggered up and made his way toward the door. Robby Rob kicked him through the opening and the old man fell to his knees, the palms of his hands skidding through the broken glass. He gave a shout of pain and Robby Rob laughed.

Hobo went to the hotdog rotisserie and looked around. Behind the counter he found a few hotdogs on the floor. He snatched them up and beat them on the counter. Then he shoved them into his mouth and began to chew methodically, pulling bits of debris out of his mouth from time to time. He scanned about the store and along the floor. The place had been trashed, most of the shelves were knocked over.

The glass doors to the refrigerator units were all broken. He kicked at some of the debris near the units and found an unbroken bottle of beer in the mess. He picked it up and opened it. He drank from it heavily and let out a long belch, then sighed in satisfaction.

"We gotta find somethin' a lot better than this, Hobo, we ain't gonna last long," Robby Rob said, his hand down the back of his pants, scratching his butt crack.

"You right 'bout that. Maybe we go find some old grandma's house, move in for a while," Hobo said grinning. His stained and rotted teeth held bits of hotdogs.

"Let's see what we can find here and let's go door ta door and find us a place ta squat. Maybe have a little fun with granny." Robby Rob laughed hysterically and rubbed his crotch.

Hobo laughed as well, and thought it was a good idea. And the more he thought about it, the better he liked the idea. He found a plastic bag and rummaged through the garbage on the floor. When he found bits of food and edible garbage, he threw it into the bag. He didn't find any more beer. Perhaps their next home would have something.

He turned in time to see Robby Rob pissing into the open refrigeration unit. He had his dick in one hand and a large pretzel in the other, chewing on it. Hobo walked past, snatched the pretzel and shoved most of it in his mouth.

"Hey man, what the hell you done that for? I'm hungry," Robby Rob yelled, turning his body, still urinating.

"Ya should have done eat it already, dumbass." Hobo laughed and walked out of the store. He stopped and smelled his fingers. They smelled like shit. He wiped them absently on his pants and went to the truck.

Ж

Dr. Lee sat at her desk in her office, looking at her charts. Her eyes began to blur. She rubbed at them hard, her knuckles turning white. She'd been at the hospital so long, and she was down to only two nurses and three orderlies. Six patients had passed away the previous night, and several had been taken by family members. There was no one in the cafeteria, so she and the nurses and orderlies had made do, feeding themselves and the patients what they could.

She wondered once more about the generator, and why it hadn't turned on. She looked out the window, it was dark and she saw no lights anywhere. Her penlight was starting to lose its glow. She sat back and looked up into the dark ceiling.

She jerked hard when her door burst open. She couldn't see the face, but she could see the silhouette of a young man, thin and gangly.

"Doctor Katie, is that you?" a male teen's voice asked, his voice cracking.

"Alan? Is that you? What are you doing here?" Katie asked, her hand held to her chest, trying to get her racing heart under control.

"Dr. Katie, you gotta come with' me, you gotta leave now!" he cried in alarm.

"What? What's going on? Why are you here? Why do you want me to leave? Is it my parents?" Katie asked, trying to calm the boy down.

"Dr. Katie, they're coming to get you, they're gonna kill you," Alan said, grabbing her arm and tugging at her, his head on a swivel. The boy was surprisingly strong and he pulled her hard.

148

Katie began to walk toward the door, then reached and grabbed her leather doctor's bag and the fading penlight. She flashed the light around the room, then let Alan pull her along. "We need to swing by the emergency room on the way out, and who is coming to kill me?" Katie asked, thinking the boy was being a bit overdramatic, but knowing he was in a real panic.

"I'll tell ya when we get to my grampa's truck, we ain't got no time for the emergency room," Alan said stridently, his long, gangly legs eating up the distance.

"We need to swing by the emergency room, I mean it," Katie insisted, wondering what was going on. The boy's panic beginning to affect her, she could feel her body responding and the small tremors that were beginning to move through her body.

She was jerked roughly in the direction of the ER, her short legs trying to keep up with the teen. Alan's breathing had become a harsh kind of sobbing and she began to pick up more of the panic that radiated from him. Her heart rate was increasing now, and it was becoming painful as it slammed into her chest.

Sweat began to lace her body, and her legs trembled as their steps led them to the ER. By the time they entered the trauma unit, her legs felt like limp noodles and she had to hold on to things so she wouldn't collapse.

Katie ran over to several cabinets, nearly stumbling. She pulled her keys from her pocket and unlocked the drawers, taking vials and needles out. Opening her valise, she swept the vials and needles into it. Then she filled the bag with gauze, antiseptic wipes, and other medical paraphernalia.

Alan's insistent tugs became more violent when they heard the roar of engines.

"They're here, we gotta get!" Alan cried, his fear filling the room.

Katie allowed herself to be led away, and ran hard to keep up with Alan. Her mouth was now cotton dry, and fear numbed her brain. Her body had taken over and the flight response was in full swing. It wasn't blind panic, but it was damned close to it.

They headed to the north exit and burst through the door. He dragged her across the pavement to the truck that was parked by the exit. He opened the passenger side door and slung her bodily into the truck. "Keep down for the love of God Almighty," Alan hissed, and slammed the door.

He jumped into the driver's seat and started the truck and raced out of the hospital parking area. His headlights were off, but when Katie peeked over the dash, she saw several trucks pull up to the ER entry doors. She saw the shadowed figures of men with weapons rushing into the hospital. Alan's truck turned violently onto a side road and she fell to the floorboards. She crawled back onto the seat and tried to pull the seatbelt, but it wouldn't budge.

"You can sit up now, we're well away," Alan said, his voice calmer, but she heard the tremor in it.

Katie sat up and held on to the armrest of the door. The truck swayed back and forth wildly, then straightened out. He switched the headlights on and slowed a bit, weaving in and out of residential streets.

"What's going on, Alan, what has happened?" Katie asked, trying to slow her heart, her own voice sounding strident.

"I ain't know how to tell ya, but them men done killed your folks, Dr. Katie," Alan said, sorrow heavy in his voice, a sob choking him off.

Katie stared at the young man, his face dark in the cab of the truck. She had to play his words over again before they registered, then her heart dropped into her stomach. Cold washed through her body, chilling her to the bone. "What?!" she cried, her voice bouncing around the cab of the truck.

"Ma'am, the KKK done showed up and dragged your ma and pa outa the house and killed them. They burned your house down, ma'am. My grandpa told me to come fetch ya," Alan said, now crying as well. Katie could see his body shaking violently, as was hers.

"Where are we going, Alan?" she asked numbly. Hot tears slid down her face and she wiped at them with an unsteady hand.

"I don't know, Ma'am, I was just told ta get you outta that hospital," Alan said.

It was silent in the truck as Alan drove around the neighborhoods, weaving in and out slowly. It was dark in the houses except for a candle here or there holding the darkness at bay. Katie let the tears fall unnoticed down her face and she wiped her nose absently with her sleeve as she leaned her head against the window. The vibration from the truck bumped at her head. Once more she wiped absently at her nose.

"Can you take me to my friend's house? Do you have enough gas?" Katie asked the boy.

"Yes'm I can take you anywhere you wanna go, got a full tank," Alan said, his voice finally calming.

Ж

Clay looked around. There were no other homes in sight. He sighed heavily. The last house he'd gone to had made the hair rise on his arms. He'd backed away and left immediately. It had been a ramshackle little place with mismatched boards and siding with large gaps; a poor house. There was a haze of stink around the house, unwashed and nasty, mixed with abject hopelessness.

There were many poor in Appalachia, in the mountains and especially around the mining towns. The people in that house were dirt poor, wretchedly so. His own family had been very poor, he had a brother and sister, and they'd shared one bedroom. His home was clean, though, his mother had made sure. His father had been a miner and had been hurt in an accident. He received disability, it wasn't much, but it did allow their family to live.

His brother had gone into the Marines and was stationed over in California. His sister had married a good man and they had moved to North Carolina some years back. He knew they were both happy. He laughed; he'd be happy if he could find a place to lay his head. Brian looked at him and cocked his head at Clay's laughter. Clay grinned down at the dog.

The man who had come to the door was thin, emaciated, and gray. His hollowed eyes looked through Clay, and the man neither spoke nor indicated he even knew Clay was there in front of him. He heard moaning in the back of the house and Clay had shivered and he'd turned on his heels and gotten away from the hovel, not even looking behind.

Clay and Brian had turned up another drive, but the house there had been roofless. So, they had continued their trek to Beattyville. The light was quickly fading and Clay didn't want to walk down the dark road. He'd have to spend the night in the woods again, though at least it wouldn't be raining.

He thought about sleeping in one of the abandoned vehicles, but didn't want to be caught inside unawares. He and Brian could just find a comfy patch of grass, away from the road.

He walked a little farther and found a break in a cluster of oak saplings. He stepped off the paved road and walked a little distance into the woods. The long shadows followed him into the forest, the birds quieting down as he passed them. He heard the soft burble of water a little bit from the road and followed the sound.

There was a small brook, and it looked wonderful, cool and sweet. It was fast flowing. He'd grown up drinking from brooks like this since he could walk. He didn't worry about any problems with microbes or aquatic parasites. He slowed and looked around and listened, it was quiet in the woods, and he saw nothing threatening. Then he heard the loud snap of a branch breaking.

CHAPTER FIFTEEN

Clay jerked around, bringing his gun up in a rapid fluid motion. He crouched and looked around. Through a large bush, that shook with his passage, came Brian. The dog was smiling with a dead chipmunk in his jaws, his tail wagging madly.

Clay dropped his arm and clutched his chest with his other hand, his heart still slamming into his chest. "Oh Lord, baby Jesus, you scared the hell out of me Brian," Clay scolded the dog, who was still grinning and wagging his tail. Clay shook his head and holstered his weapon.

Clay breathed in deeply and then blew out the stress. He shook his head and laughed. At least Brian would have a little extra food, though he didn't want to watch the dog eat it. He watched the dog disappear back into the bush and Clay walked over to the brook and set the backpack down.

He looked around the area once more. The birds had started singing again and the insects were buzzing. It was quite peaceful, and Clay felt his heart rate begin to slow.

Brian was at the brook in a blink, lapping up the water quickly. Clay squatted down beside the dog and cut his eyes to him. He hoped the dog had eaten the chipmunk. He looked in the backpack for the empty bottles. He was glad he'd held onto the plastic water bottles, as they were coming in handy.

He filled one and quickly drank it down, then refilled it once more and drank more slowly. It was sweet and cold, and felt good going down his throat. It almost ached, it was so pleasant. He then washed his face, splashing the cool water over himself. It had been a long, hot day walking.

Clay took off his shoes and socks next, then put his tired hot feet into the brook, rubbing the soles of his feet on the nubby small pebbles on the bottom. He groaned in bliss, his head tilting back, and closed his eyes. He could hear Brian still lapping at the water.

The tree frogs began their nightly songs, soon joined by the crickets. High in the branches, he heard a Veery thrush, its rolling trill weaving in and out of the leaves of the trees. Then he heard a mockingbird calling out.

Looking around, he saw a low spot that had lush grass growing. He got up from the ground, groaning loudly. His body was tired and sore. He walked over barefooted and sat on the lush clearing. He took off his tactical vest, as well as his holster, then removed his uniform shirt and laid it aside. His white undershirt was damp, and he was sure it smelled like hell. He was on his third day of walking and with no shower, he was sure he was ripe. The night before, it had poured the rain.

He remembered sleeping with his siblings, water dripping on him at night when it was a hard rain. The roof leaked badly. The room had been so small, there was nowhere to run. He'd sneak out and sleep in the living room. He wasn't sure why the memories were coming; maybe too much quiet time on his hands.

He stripped down and went back to the brook. Squatting, he scooped up a handful of the fine pebbles. Standing in the stream, he began to rub the small rocks over his body and under his arms, using the fine grit to clean himself. He shivered. It felt good after a hot day. He rinsed and rinsed again.

By the time he was finished, his teeth were chattering, though the air was still warm. He took his uniform shirt and dried himself with it, then took it to the stream, along with his undershirt, and washed them out. He also washed his socks. He squeezed and wrung the clothing out, getting as much water out as he could.

Walking back to the grassy area, he snapped the shirt smartly and laid it over a bush to dry overnight, following it up with the undershirt. He put his pants back on, then pulled out the emergency blanket and laid it on the ground. He set his shoes beside the backpack.

He'd helped his mother wash clothes at a small stream in the back of their yard. It had been too expensive to go to the laundromat, and they could not afford a washing machine. Their life had been hard and there wasn't much food, but his mother had managed to make it work. She grew a small garden and had two hens. School helped some with free lunches. His father hadn't wanted to beg, but Clay's mother had put her foot down.

Clay pulled out the last of his beef jerky and half a granola bar. He also poured the last of the dog food into Brian's bowl. He added a little water to it to make a gravy, feeling terrible that he didn't have more food for Brian. At least the dog had found a chipmunk, small as

157

that was. He broke a little off his beef jerky and added it to the dog food.

"Sorry Brian, that is the last of your food, and not sure when you'll get more. Hopefully you can catch another chipmunk or a squirrel, just no skunks please. Maybe tomorrow we'll get lucky and find someone that will feed us. Enjoy it while you have it, boy, 'cause it might be a while until our next meal," Clay said, eating his food slowly. He drank the water, and it was sweet.

He heaved a sigh and lay back, using the backpack as a pillow. He continued to chew his food slowly, making it last, and listened to the night's serenade and the susurrus of the wind weaving in and out of the canopy. It was a tranquil spot and he was glad he'd found it.

He'd not been this hungry since he was a kid, and he felt his stomach devouring the food he nibbled on. He'd grown into a big man and he had sworn to himself he'd never go hungry again. Up until now, he'd kept that promise.

He remembered his mother making grits and macaroni and greens; it was filling. She had fried up a piece of chicken for their father, but had let the children smell the chicken and eat their food first before their father ate the chicken. They'd almost felt like they were eating the meat, but it wasn't the same. It was rare that they ate meat unless Clay or his brother shot a squirrel.

Years later, he'd told a Navy buddy about it, and had laughed at the thought of sniffing fried chicken and eating grits. His friend hadn't laughed, and Clay had seen the sorrow deep within his friend's eyes. For Clay, it had been normal, but he supposed it really hadn't been.

In his home, Clay now kept shelves filled with foodstuffs. His refrigerator was always full and the freezer was packed as well. He made sure he had meat with his dinner every night. He wouldn't go so far as to call himself a hoarder, but the food in his house could keep him fed for well over a year easily.

He never wanted to live that way again, hand to mouth. He felt his eyes tear up at the memories of his mother struggling to feed her children. He shook his head to dispel the melancholy.

The light began to fade faster, the shadows drowning out the sun, and he called Brian over. The dog curled up by his side. He took the emergency blanket and shook it out, profoundly glad he had brought it. He wrapped the blanket around him and lay on the ground.

The mountains got cold at night, and with the sun sinking, he could feel the air cooling rapidly. If he were home, he wouldn't mind. He had quilts on his bed, made by his mother, that would keep him toasty. His eyes grew heavy from the exertion of a long day walking. He closed his eyes and let his body relax into slumber.

Ж

Harry sat in the swing, Willene beside him, while Marilyn sat in the rocker, with Monroe, who was snoring softly, in her lap. Boggy was out in back with his LED flashlight, making a round on the property, checking the barn and the chicken lot. It was pitch-black but for dots of illumination in the distance, caused by multiple fires. Traces of smoke now lingered in the air constantly, thankfully not heavily so.

Harry brought the NVGs up to his eyes and scanned the hill below and tree line. Seeing nothing, he put them down between himself and Willy. The dog was somewhere on the porch, asleep, his soft snores lost in the buzz of the night insects.

"I'm surprised we've not heard more gunfire; it's been three days now," Willene said to no one in particular.

"I'm sure someone is shooting someone. Probably the closer they are to town the less chance we'd hear anything. Shooting up in the mountains causes the sound to bounce around," Harry said as he took a drink of warm sweet tea.

"At least it's been quiet here," Marilyn said softly.

Everyone sat up suddenly; there was a light in the far distance, headlights. With no other artificial lights around, it was like a beacon was screaming their way. Harry stood and waved everyone to sit. He heard Boggy come around the side of the house.

"Turn off your flashlight, Boggy, they'll be able to see it clearly. Everyone, stay still. They may just pass by. Let's see what's going to happen," Harry ordered softly.

The group watched as the lights drew nearer, swerving in and out of view as the vehicle wound around the curves of the mountain. The vehicle's speed appeared nominal, so it took a couple minutes for the car to head to the curve in the road that led to the drive.

The vehicle passed by and a collective sigh was released into the air.

"That was close," Boggy said softly, his voice trembling as though he didn't want the driver to hear him.

"There are functioning vehicles still, and hopefully, with the barricade in place, no one will know the house is here at night," Harry said.

"Shit," Willy said, and everyone looked to her, though they could barely see her.

"The vehicle is coming back," Marilyn said, her voice tense.

Looking down, the lights could be seen making a U-turn up the road. It retraced its path, this time very slowly. Then it pulled to a stop in front of the blockade. They saw someone get out, and Harry brought up the NVGs to take a look. He saw what looked like a young thin man, and then a woman got out of the passenger's side of the truck.

"Looks like some kid and a woman," Harry said and, pulling his Glock, began walking down the hill. He took his time, as he didn't want to slip on the damp grass.

"Willene? It's me, Katie. Can I come up with my friend, Alan?" a woman called.

"She's okay, Harry, bring her up," Willene called down.

"Got it, sis," Harry said. He took his small LED flashlight and turned it on.

The woman and young man wove their way through the blind. Harry almost laughed as the woman got hung up on the framework, her white lab coat getting caught on a nail. Alan was trying to help her when he reached them. He reached over the young man's shoulder and pulled the white lab coat from the nail, an audible rip sounding.

"My coat," Katie said, her voice low and soft.

"It'll mend," Harry said and, taking the woman by the arm, led her up the hill.

"Are you Willy's brother?" Katie asked.

"Yes, I take it you're Dr. Katie? Willy has mentioned you a few times," Harry said, grinning.

"Yes, and this is my neighbor's grandson, Alan. He came to the hospital. He told me the KKK has killed my parents," the sorrow in Katie's voice caused Harry to stop in mid stride. He looked down at the doctor. Her mouth was trembling, holding back the emotions.

"I'm sorry. Let's get you up to the house and we'll sort this out," Harry said softly, and started once more up the hill, Alan following behind.

Willene met them at the bottom of the steps and Katie pulled loose from Harry and ran the short distance to hug Willene, bursting into tears as she did so. Harry watched as his sister led the petite woman into the house. Everyone followed.

"I'll go take Monroe up to our room," Marilyn said, and she turned and took the still-sleeping Monroe into the house.

The kitchen had a candle burning on the table and everyone sat down. Willene took the still-warm pot of coffee off the stove and took cups out of the cupboard.

162

"How did all this happen, Katie?" Willene asked gently, setting a cup in front of the woman.

Katie looked over to Alan, and the young man sat up straighter. Everyone looked at him, and he blushed a little, his eyes darting like someone caught with their hand in the cookie jar.

The teen gulped a couple times, took a sip of the coffee Willene had poured him, and settled down. "I was sittin' in my house with my grandpa, and then I heard this truck come a screechin' up next door. Those KKK men, they done had them sheets on their head. They plumb scared me bad, but then I heard Dr. Katie's parents just a yellin' and carrying on, and her momma crying," Alan said, and then choked up, a sob breaking his voice.

Katie joined in the sobbing, and for a moment the room was filled with their weeping. Willene put her arm around her friend and hugged her. Harry got up and fetched a box of tissues from the living room and brought them back to the kitchen.

Harry placed his hand on the teen's shoulder and squeezed gently. He looked over to Boggy and saw the boy's eyes tearing up. This wasn't good, the KKK rearing its ugly head. He felt a chill running down his body, dread beginning to build in him.

Clearing his voice, Alan continued. "They was just laughing and carrying on. They were sayin' how this is the white man's time, an' it was the white man's town. Ain't no colored people, ain't no Chinese, no gays, no A-rabs, gonna live in their town. They said your folks was North Koreans, and communists and they caused this whole mess." Alan wiped his eyes and nose with a tissue.

The boy picked up the coffee cup with shaking hands and took a sip. Harry looked around the room, shaking his head. This was unreal. Not only had the world's power come down, but now the goddamn KKK was trying to take over the town and kill every non-white.

They were the domestic terrorists of the United States, pretty much the oldest domestic terrorists the United States had. It was too bad the government hadn't taken their threat more seriously. The politicians screamed free speech, but the Ku Klux Klan was built on terrorism.

"They done shot your momma and daddy Dr. Katie, I'm real sorry. I didn't know what to do, or how to stop them. Two men tried ta stop them, the KKK just shot them dead in the street. My grandpa said they'd kill me if I got out there. I'm dang sorry Dr. Katie," Alan ended, looking down at his hands as the tears fell onto the table, his bony shoulders shaking.

"These people, these KKK, they killed my parents because they thought they were North Korean? My parents are American, like me. They were born in Lexington, for Christ's sakes. Then they kill anyone trying to help them?" Katie choked out, using a napkin to wipe her nose and eyes.

"I don't think it would matter, Katie. These men would clearly hurt or kill anyone on their short list. And anyone standing in their way or helping the hunted. It sounds like the mayor is taking over," Willene said

164

angrily, her hands wrapping around her coffee cup in a death grip.

"How do you know it's Mayor Audrey taking over?" Harry asked.

Willene and Marilyn laughed harshly at the same time. Marilyn had just come down in time to hear the last of Harry's question. Harry looked at the women, then at Boggy, who was silent, his eyes watching the people around him. The boy's eyes were filled with unshed tears and fear. Boggy may be young, but he knew what the hate of the KKK could do, Harry was sure.

"Mayor Audrey and Sheriff Yates are high up in the KKK organization," Marilyn said, dabbing her nose with a tissue. "It is rumor, mind you, but I'd not put it past them."

"I thought the KKK was pretty much shut down," Harry said, shaking his head.

"No Harry, it's goin' strong and alive. I suspect they keep it on the down low. I'd watch my back every time. Those boys are mean," Boggy said. "My granny said she'd had a couple run-ins with them boys. Said they's bad'uns. Special when she was young."

"With all the checks and balances, and phones that video everything, the mayor and the sheriff were kept in check. They didn't want any lawsuit, and for the most part have kept their rhetoric to themselves," Marilyn added.

"They've also kept their people on a short leash; that is, until now," Willene said, anger lacing her voice, her mouth hard and turned down.

165

"Now those checks and balances are gone, along with the law," Marilyn said, her voice flat and angry.

"What we gonna do, Harry?" Boggy asked, fear and hope warring in his eyes as he looked at Harry, the coffee cup clutched to his chest like a shield.

"I don't know. I don't want to go out looking for a fight, but I won't run from them. With Earl down and hurt, there are only five adults here, and I'm sure the KKK has plenty of men who will be glad to end all of us," Harry said as he looked into his cup, a frown on his face. "We need to think and plan this out. There isn't much we can do unless they bring this fight to us."

"Katie, you can stay with us now. If you go back anywhere near town, those animals will kill you," Willene said, placing her arm around the doctor.

"Yes, Katie, you'll need to stay here with us, I agree with Willene, I don't think it is safe. We are far enough away that we shouldn't encounter too much trouble. We are well armed," Harry said, looking around the table at each face.

Katie looked at the twins, her eyes tearing up. She then reached over and grabbed Willene and Harry's hands. Her mouth trembled as she tried to smile through the tears that streamed down her face. "Thank you so much for your kindness. Can you tell me what has happened? Why is the power out? I think I know, but I'm hoping I'm wrong," Katie said.

"We think it might have been an EMP via a coronal eruption. Now, the reason I think it might be a coronal eruption is that our grandfather said it was,"

Harry said, and raised a hand when Katie opened her mouth to say something.

"I know what you are thinking, but my grandfather was dying. It is said by our native American ancestors that when a person is close to death, they have one foot in this world and one foot in the next." He looked at Willene, who nodded. "My grandfather also knew about my girlfriend in Germany, and knew her name," Harry said, looking at Willene.

Willene sat forward. "Girlfriend?"

A smile trembled on Harry's lips as he tried to stifle the pain. "I had been dating Franziska Gnodtke for over a year. She's in Germany. I'd not told anyone about her but had planned to. Peapot knew who she was, and told me she would be fine. He also said that this mess was because of the sun."

Harry looked around at the faces, and noted the hair rising on everyone's arms. He could see the goosebumps clearly in the candlelight. Alan shrank a little in his chair, his shoulders going up toward his ears.

Harry cleared his throat. "Anyway, I think what has happened was caused by a solar coronal event, some kind of eruption, or a massive solar storm or something. I think it hit the whole world. I don't think we will get power any time soon," Harry finished, shrugging helplessly.

The room was quiet for a moment, everyone taking in the revelation. Alan shifted in his chair, then stood. "Reckon I'd better skedaddle, get back to my grandpa, I think he's gonna be worried. I'll keep an ear out, and maybe if I hear anything important, I'll come back. I think I got enough gas for a couple more trips."

Harry slapped the teen on the shoulders, intending to lead him out of the kitchen.

"Thank you, Alan, you saved my life," Katie said, getting up. She walked over to the teen and hugged him. The tall gawky teen glowed red in the dim light, an embarrassed grin on his homely face.

Alan waved farewell to the women and shook Boggy's hand. He bumped into the table and it shook violently. He grinned, embarrassed, and made his way out of the kitchen, Harry following.

Harry led the way down the hill and helped Alan through the barricade. Alan reached inside the truck and drew out Katie's bag. He handed it over to Harry.

"Drive carefully and don't say anything to anyone, not even your grandfather. Tonight, didn't happen. Tell your grandfather that Dr. Katie wasn't at the hospital. That way, if anyone asks him, he can truthfully say he doesn't know," Harry instructed the young man.

Alan's head nodded like a bobble head, and he slowly pulled away and headed down the winding road. For a few minutes, Harry stood and watched the red tail lights heading out of sight. There was no moon, but the stars were bright. Harry looked up into the night sky.

The brilliant stars had never shone so bright here before, uninterrupted by the ever-present glow of towns or cities. It was a breathtaking sight, and Harry knew that the natural beauty could be marred by greedy, evil humans. He didn't know what was coming, but he

knew something was; there was no doubt in his mind.
They had to get ready, really ready.

CHAPTER SIXTEEN

Mayor Audrey sat back in his chair, a large smile on his lips. Across from him was Sheriff Yates, who was smoking a cigar and blowing smoke rings above his head. There were five other men in the room: Officer Grady, Officer Learn and Officer Smalls, and two new recruits.

"Y'all boys did a damn good job," Audrey said with a yellow smile. "Most every non-white is now out of our town, one way or another." He crowed with laughter at the thought.

"You boys ever find that North Korean doctor, Katie Lee?" Tate asked, his light blue eyes moving from man to man.

"No sir, we asked her commie parents, but they didn't say nothin', just that gook shit. We had ta kill a couple of do-gooders, they were trying to step into our business," Grady said, a sneer on his face and his sandy eyebrows pulled down.

"We got to the hospital, and looked around, but couldn't find her. Just a couple nurses an' orderlies. We questioned them, but they didn't know nothing."

"Ah well, she'll turn up somewhere," Audrey said, the smile still on his face. His teeth looked like large yellow chiclets. "Y'all did a fine job and got lots of good Christian white folk to bolster our numbers and protect what's ours." Audrey looked at the new men, his thick brows going up. The men shuffled their feet, eyes fixed on the floor.

"Yes sir, and we got thirty people all together. Some is ex-military, except they was dishonorably discharged," Officer Vern Small said, and shrugged,

Mayor Audrey looked at the short thin man. He knew Vern to be a vicious little bastard.

"That's okay, son, we can work with 'em," Yates said dismissively.

"Sir, Clay Patterson ain't come back from Lexington yet. What do we do when he gets back?" Grady asked, chewing his lower lip, his hand stroking the butt of his weapon in its holster.

"Well, if he shows up, we just take care of him like I did Deets." Sheriff Yates smiled and blew a plume of fragrant smoke into the air.

"Officer Grady, I want you to gather your people, start on the outskirts of town and work your way in. Go house to house and confiscate weapons," the mayor announced, sitting up straight in his chair. "I don't want to worry about our citizens getting too rowdy. Besides, with our large police force, folks don't got to worry about protecting themselves. Y'all got their backs."

"Next, you need to check for food and usable supplies. I don't want your people to take everything, just tell them we just need a bit. I don't want these folks getting up in arms about it." Audrey's face dead serious, his eyes drilling into Grady's. "Tell them we will make more food available at a determined date. Do not rough them up. You are to be polite and courteous, do I make myself clear?" Mayor Audrey ordered firmly.

171

He looked at each man and then the sheriff. At the sheriff's nod, he continued.

"If they refuse on either account, just take their names and we will deal with them later. For now, we want everyone to feel good about our new police force. We want them to feel safe and we want them on *our* side. We are in this for the long haul," he concluded.

The men exited the room with their orders. Mayor Audrey leaned back in his chair and propped his feet up on his desk. He clacked his small shoes together. "Life sure is looking white, and right." He laughed hard.

Sheriff Yates joined in the laughter. The room rang with harsh hilarity as both men felt the power of the plans they'd made and the fact that things were going great. So far, there had been very few snags. The disappearance of the doctor was troublesome, but not really important.

Rupert Audrey and Danny Yates had opened a new and sweeping chapter of the KKK in their town. All townspeople were welcome to join. They had posted notices announcing one and all were welcome into the klavern.

They had set a bounty for turning in anyone who wasn't white and wasn't a Christian and most certainly anyone who wasn't heterosexual. It was a sweeping plan to ferret out those who tried to hide from the long arm of the law. There were also added incentives.

"For the first time in my life, I ain't gonna apologize for my lineage. I can tell the world I'm with the KKK and that all non-whites should fear me,"

172

Rupert said, relighting a cigar. He pulled on the stogy and puffed.

"I can remember my grandpappy telling me about his grandpappy being in the KKK. They were real proud and real powerful back then. In the last thirty years, our power and influence have gone down the toilet," Yates said, a sour look on his face.

"Don't I know it. But we will rebuild. We now hold the power and the might, and the right on our side," Audrey said, giving the sheriff a toothy grin.

Both men sat silent, smiling to themselves. Outside, random shots were fired in the distance. "You'll need to get that under control. I don't want my citizens feeling fearful. They need to know they are secure in our hands," Rupert said.

"You got it, Mayor. I'll take care of it. That sure was a good plan of yours to put them undesirables to work for us, that is what ya call free labor," Yates said, smiling.

"They had it right the first time with slavery; we need to get back to simpler times. We're at the top of the food chain now, and I plan to stay there," Rupert crowed with laughter.

Ж

Katie lay in the bed weeping, her hand covering her mouth to silence the moans. Willene was on duty, her soft steps creaking on the worn wooden boards of the porch. Katie couldn't comprehend the magnitude of what had happened. Not just the coronal event that knocked their world back a few hundred years, but the evil and hate that had killed her parents.

Her sweet parents, who'd been so kind and given everything for her to go to medical school. They had been loving parents, and they didn't deserve it; they didn't deserve to be killed.

She sat up, knowing she couldn't sleep. She smoothed back the mass of heavy black hair and secured it with an elastic tie. Her eyes hurt, puffy and swollen from the crying. She got up and walked to the window.

The shy moon had come out and she looked out over the mountains, dark against the lighter, starlit sky. She'd been at this house many times over the years, but she'd never stayed overnight. The bedroom was small and neat. It held a daybed, a small dresser, and a wash stand. It was very old fashioned.

She picked up the flashlight she'd been given and shone it around the room. There was faded floral wallpaper, reminiscent of the early nineteenth century. The wash stand had a beautiful ceramic carafe that looked like it also belonged in the nineteenth century. The curtains at the open window were white with eyelets around the edges, and there was the small closet she'd put her valise into.

She had no clothing, except what she'd worn for the last three days. Willene and Marilyn had given her some of their clothing, and Willene had given her a bowl of hot water, soap, and a towel. Their kindness touched Katie deeply. They were like sisters she'd never had.

Katie had cleaned up and changed into a long t-shirt. She'd laughed, because it came down to her shins. It must have been one of Harry's old shirts. It was very large, but very comfortable. The faded lettering said *An Army of One.*

She quietly made her way downstairs; the light illuminated her way to the porch. She opened the screen door and, stepping out into the cool of the night, she turned off the flashlight. Katie drew in a deep breath and reveled in the freshness on her heated face. She saw Willene coming around the corner of the house and lifted a hand.

"Can't sleep?" Willene asked.

"No. I keep thinking about my parents. They didn't deserve that hate, that evil cruelty," Katie whispered, her voice catching in her throat.

"No, they didn't. They were the sweetest people I knew, and they always made me feel welcome," Willene said, a soft smile in her voice.

"What are we going to do, Willy? How can these people do this and get away with it?" Katie asked, her voice filled with fear and her hands twisted each other into locked finger knots.

"I don't know. We are so far away from town, and though we have plenty of guns, I don't know what is going on there now, how many KKK there are, or even who they are. What would happen if we went into town? I think Harry, Earl, and Boggy want to go take a look for themselves. Earl is down right now; he was nearly beaten to death by some of his so-called friends," Willene said.

"Boggy is black. Do you think that's a good idea, to take him into town?" Katie asked.

175

"I guess that would be up to Boggy. But we will have to wait and see. Right now, it feels like we are paralyzed, unable to do much," Willene complained.

Katie looked around the hills that surrounded the farmhouse. She could see the tinge of blush of the coming dawn over the mountains to the east. It was peaceful, unlike the turmoil roiling in her soul. She took a shuddering breath and let out a heavy sigh. She knew she had to move past all this. The horror and the hate would eat her alive if she let it.

"I know my parents are in heaven now, and with this world going to hell, they may well be in a better place," Katie said, wiping at the tears sliding down her cheeks.

Willene walked over and wrapped her arms around her friend, hugging her. "Tomorrow, or rather, later today, we will work on setting up more alarms in the woods surrounding the house, traps and tripwires. We also need to expand our garden, plant more veggies. You might want to get some rest if you can," Willene suggested, patting Katie on the back.

"I'm sure you're right. I feel so restless. Thank you again for allowing me to live here. The room is lovely," she said.

"No thanks needed, you are a welcome addition. If you don't mind, maybe later check on Earl? We helped him as best we could," Willene asked.

Katie laughed a little. "I'm sure you and Marilyn did fine, but I will be glad to check him. I'll be as helpful as I can. I love gardening, and I'm a great cook as well."

176

"I'm glad you are here. The more hands, the better off we will be. It looks like we will have to take care of ourselves in more ways than one. Those lawless bastards can't get away with what they are doing. Somehow, some way, we will get them ousted," Willene said, a mulish tilt to her jaw.

Katie laughed again. She knew that mulish look, having seen it many times at the hospital with a difficult case or a difficult patient. Willene usually got her way, only because the woman never gave up.

Katie bid Willene a good night, albeit a short one, and she headed into the house. She didn't need her flashlight, now able to make out objects in the gloom. She climbed the stairs as quietly as she could, but they still squeaked softly beneath her bare feet.

Ж

The sun had been up for a few hours, and Clay was already sweating. His stomach growled loudly, and he knew Brian was feeling the pangs as well. They had plenty of water; they'd had their fill and refilled his water bottles.

"You know, Brian, you can always go catch a squirrel," he told the dog. Brian's tail wagged, but he kept by Clay's side, sniffing the ground.

They'd come across a couple abandoned cars, and looked through them, but found nothing to eat. He was starting to get a niggling feeling far back in his brain, about the cars he'd found abandoned and the loss of power at Pop's home.

Whether he couldn't puzzle it out or he didn't want to puzzle it out for fear of knowing exactly what was

177

going on, he didn't know. He tried not to think about it, but the farther he walked and the more abandoned vehicles he came across, the more the nagging thought tried to penetrate the front of his thoughts.

Brian whined, and Clay looked down and petted the dog. "Sorry boy, I am hoping we can find a house. We have maybe another day before we get home. I'm surprised we've not seen anyone," he told his partner. The dog looked up at him and gave a doggy grin. Clay grinned back.

In the distance, he heard the heavy rumble of a vehicle coming, the first he'd heard in days. His heart leapt with joy; at last, a ride home. He turned to await the oncoming vehicle.

He wiped away the sweat once more from his face and stood over to the side of the road, his back to the forest. The other side of the road was a drop off the low mountain side. He shifted back and forth on his feet, excitement building in him at the thought of getting home and eating a real meal at last.

An old red rusted Ford drove around a hairpin curve, the windshield thick with dust and pollen. Clay could see two men in the front, and there looked to be three or more in the back of the truck. He didn't care; he would ride on the hood if it meant getting back home. As the truck drew near, it began to slow, and Clay smiled and began to wave his hand, hailing them.

The truck came to a stop about ten yards away and Clay began to walk forward toward them. He was about to tell them how happy he was to see them, when one of the men in the back of the truck bed stood up and aimed a shotgun at him. Clay stopped, frozen, and Brian began to growl, the hair along his back standing stiffly up.

"Boy, where y'all think you're going?" the man asked. He was greasy looking and dirty.

Clay took in the filthy wifebeater undershirt, the tattoos that covered his chest and arms. He also noticed, even from that distance, that the man sported a large swastika tattoo on his shoulder. The man spat a stream of brown substance to the ground, then jumped down from the truck bed.

Clay's hand fell, and brushed his weapon, but he didn't grab it yet. "I'm Officer Patterson, of the Beattyville Police Department. My cruiser died some ways back, and if it isn't too much, can y'all give me a ride back to town? I'd be much obliged," Clay called out in a strong voice.

Clay felt as though ants were crawling all over his body, the warning bells screaming "Run, run, run." His eyes took in everything about the men, and it wasn't adding up to anything good. So far, the other men remained in the truck. But Clay knew it wouldn't take a skinny minute for all of them to be out.

All the men in the truck began to laugh, an ugly laugh. The primitive hair prickled along Clay's body. Clay scanned around him quickly. Things were about to go sideways.

CHAPTER SEVENTEEN

Clay was profoundly grateful for his police training. He jerked around and ran into the woods, calling after Brian. Lowering his upper torso by bending at the waist, he ran in a zigzag pattern. The explosion behind him was loud, and his body jerked as leaves and small branches blew up next to him.

He crouched even lower, making himself a smaller target. Brian could be heard running beside him, and he kept running as more gunshots were fired in his directions. When he could, he changed directions, trying to keep the noise down as he went. He hoped they were making more noise than he was.

Brian drew abreast of Clay and then passed him, Clay was running as fast as he could while dodging the low hanging branches and bushes. He was also mindful of rocks and roots. He could hear his pursuers gaining on him.

Another booming shot, this time closer, and he felt the searing hot pain rip through his left shoulder and side. He felt the shot peppering on the back of his vest as well. They had shot him with buckshot; had they been closer, he was sure it would have killed him.

His breathing became hard and labored, and his mouth was as dry as the sand in a heat-scorched desert. All he could hear now was the pounding of his heart and the harsh breath coming from his open mouth. His eyes felt dry as well.

Clay's dark eyes darted wildly, looking for an escape or hiding place. He heard another shot, and dodged left, then began an uphill run, the adrenaline taking him higher. In some distant part of his brain, he was glad he'd kept up his running since leaving the Navy years ago. Though he was tired from walking for days and on little food, his muscle memory kept him upright and moving forward.

He could no longer see Brian ahead of him, and all he could think of was that he was glad they wouldn't kill his dog. If he could find a good place to settle, he could return fire, but they had kept up with him until now. He could hear their shouts down the hill from him, and then his skin turned cold.

The baying of a hound dog echoed up the mountain. They had a dog, and there was no place to hide from a hound. He had to go to ground and get into a defensive position. It was like a nightmare from a really bad movie, like one he'd seen set in the 50s. This was crazy and surreal; never in his life had he encountered anything remotely this bad.

His body was screaming with pain and he thought his heart would explode. His chest shrieked in agony. He was going deeper and deeper into the dense woods, and the hound behind him was gaining ground. The deep reverberating baying followed him up the mountain, relentless.

He had to stop that hound, because no matter where he hid, it would find him. He hated killing a dog, but those bastards had set it loose on him. He found a large oak, and stopped, hiding behind it, his breath coming in heavy sobbing gasps. The large tree held him up, his body heavy against the rough bark.

His left arm felt dead, but his right arm was whole, and he drew his weapon and waited. He could hear the dog's progress and eventually saw its shape through the heavy brush. Taking aim, his hand shaking badly, he fired off and missed. Taking a deep breath, he dug deep and calmed himself, took the shot, and heard the dog yelp. He didn't know if he'd killed it, he hoped he hadn't, but he'd stopped the dog from coming after him.

He didn't linger but staggered on, now feeling the effects of the blood loss. His teeth were chattering. He continued to run up and along a deer trail, bouncing off trees and staggering. He could hear the men down the mountain screaming and shooting wildly, but Clay could no longer understand their words. Brian was somewhere ahead of him. He could hear the dog and see motion and movement far ahead, disappearing in and out of the trees and undergrowth.

He was starting to feel queasy, and dark spots floated around the perimeter of his vision. His breaths were coming in harsh gasps now, and his legs began to wobble like drunken rubber bands. He desperately searched for somewhere to hide; he knew he was about to faint, and he didn't want those bastards to find him unconscious and kill him.

He was slowing now, falling against trees, trying to keep himself upright. His hand grasped desperately at rough bark; deep scratches covered his right hand. His left arm was completely numb and he was beginning to lose feeling in his right. Clay was mindful not to leave a bloody trail. He didn't need those peckerwoods following that and finding him.

His head was pounding, and he kept swallowing, trying to keep the acid down in his gut. His gaze was drawn to a small declivity behind a thick sweet bush. He stumbled toward it, the black spots growing and coalescing. With everything left in him, Clay made it to the declivity and crawled in, turning and making sure the bush was still in place, and then everything went black.

Ж

Harry and Boggy were in the woods at the back of the farmhouse, stringing fishing line at different heights and attaching empty metal cans with pebbles inside. They also used rusted old cowbells, jingle bells and other noisy items that had been scrounged around the barn. Earl was up in his bed, recuperating from his beating. He was starting to get around better, and they'd managed to straighten out his prosthetic leg.

Willy, Marilyn, and Katie were in the garden planting more seeds, squash, zucchini, Kentucky wander beans, pink bush beans, and green peppers. They didn't have any more tomato seeds, as Willene had planted all she had in the spring. There were thirty tomato plants, covered with blooms and large green tomatoes. Once ripened, they would be canned, and some would be dehydrated.

Harry paused, wiping the sweat from his forehead. The sun was high in the clear cobalt sky and beating down on them, despite the tree's canopy. He should have brought some water, but he'd figured they'd be in

183

the shade and cooler. How wrong he'd been. He bent to pick up another reel of filament fishing line when he heard a gunshot blast. It was close to the property, if not on it.

He turned and ran toward the house. Boggy exited the woods fifty feet up the hill, likewise heading for the house. The women had also heard, and were acting similarly. Marilyn snatched Monroe up and carried him with her. Harry reached Marilyn, took Monroe from her and slung the boy over his shoulder, eliciting a shriek and a giggle from the boy.

"Willy, get upstairs with the AR15 and watch out the windows along the drive and the front of the house. Katie, do you know how to use a gun?" Harry asked.

"No, I don't, I'm sorry," she said, looking apologetic.

Harry smiled crookedly, and said, "Don't worry, we'll teach you."

"I'll take her and Monroe to the basement, and then I'll get my .38," Marilyn said.

"Okay. Me and Boggy will head to the woods," Harry said, and was interrupted by more gunshots, this time closer.

He and Boggy ran out of the house and into the woods, toward another flurry of gunshots. They separated and headed deeper into the forest. Harry could hear a dog baying and turned toward it. He jumped over logs, rocks, and bushes. He drew closer to the gunshots, then heard a dog cry out. He could hear men screaming and cursing, and picked up his pace.

184

He was heading downhill now, zeroing in on the men's voices. He brought his Glock up in a ready position. He heard the men ahead of him. He found a large rock and placed his body behind it and scanned for the men. There were six of them, five armed with hunting rifles, and one had a shotgun.

"You men, freeze! You're on my property! Put your weapons down or I will start shooting! Do it now!" Harry shouted in a harsh voice.

The men turned toward him, and one lifted his rifle. Harry shot him, the bullet punching into his chest. The other men fled, leaving their compatriot behind. Harry kept his gun up and walked carefully toward the downed man.

He looked down and saw that the man was dead. Beside him was a dog, a blue tick hound, also dead. He heard movement in the bushes behind him and Harry whirled, bringing his weapon to bear.

Boggy jerked down and screamed, "It's me!"

Harry turned back to the downed man. He was filthy, with greasy thin red hair. He wore camo cargo pants and a filthy polyester golf shirt. His hunting rifle lay beside him.

"Who the hell is he?" Harry asked, looking over at Boggy.

"I expect he's a KKK boy, look at them swastikas tattooed all over his arms an' the one on his neck. No big loss," Boggy said, turning and spitting on the ground in disgust.

"Yeah, but what the hell is he doing on my property? He and those other men were clustered

185

around the dog." Harry turned and narrowed his eyes, scanning. In the distance, he heard a truck revving its engine and then tires squealing away.

"Ain't no telling, maybe they was hunting deer or something?" Boggy guessed. He also was looking around in the dense forest, his weapon at the low ready.

Both men turned when they heard something coming through the trees. Both men raised their weapons, but lowered them when a dog came through the trees; it looked like a German shepherd mix.

Harry patted his leg and called to the dog, who came to him, tail wagging. Harry patted and rubbed the dog's head, and looked down at the collar. It was a police dog. He looked up at Boggy. "He's a police dog, and his name is Brian. Were those assholes trying to kill him? Or his handler?" he wondered aloud.

Harry squatted down. "Hey buddy, where's your policeman?" The dog tilted his head from side to side and smiled at Harry. Harry laughed and petted the dog.

"I don't think he speaks English," Boggy said laughing and reached over to pet the dog.

The dog then barked and trotted off. Harry looked at Boggy and shrugged, and began to follow the dog. Both men moved through the forest, keeping the dog in their sights. The dog turned, still smiling, and barked. He sat down and his tail wagged.

"Is Timmy in the well?" Harry asked the dog, laughing.

The dog barked again, his tail wagging harder. Harry looked over to Boggy and shrugged, unsure what to do. He looked back at the dog, then looked around the area. He scanned the trees, and bushes. His eyes were drawn to a sweet bush; the tip of a sneaker was peeking out from beneath the vegetation. He walked swiftly over, squatted down and pulled the bush aside. There he found a large, unconscious man in uniform, except for the sneakers.

"Help me, Boggy, this man's been shot! We need to get him back to the house," Harry said, waving his friend over.

Boggy came over and bent forward, looking down. "That's Clay Patterson, he be a police officer from Beattyville. You think them bad men was hunting him down?"

"It looks like it. Be careful now; you get on one side and I'll get the other side," Harry said, and they lifted the unconscious man as gently as they could. Harry whistled for the dog to follow them.

"What 'bout that dead feller back there?" Boggy asked, grunting as he shouldered the weight.

"We'll get back to that later. Let's get Officer Patterson to the house and let Katie and Willy look at him," Harry suggested, grunting as he tried to shoulder the large man.

Both Harry and Boggy were sweating profusely by the time they got to the front yard. Harry called for Katie and Willene, his voice echoing across the yard and bouncing off the house. By the time they made the steps, Willene was coming out the screen door, Katie behind her.

"That's Clay! What happened?" Katie asked, her voice rising.

187

Katie held the door open while Harry and Boggy pulled the large man into the house. They laid him down on the living room floor and Harry stepped by to let the women at the unconscious man. Marilyn came down the stairs with Katie's medical bag and Willene's emergency first aid kit.

"There was a group of men, we think they may be associated with the KKK; they must have been chasing him and shot him. When I confronted them, one of them made to shoot at me and I killed him before the rest turned and ran away. We heard their truck peel out and I think they are gone," Harry said, wiping the sweat that was pouring down his heated face.

"Oh my God, what animals these people are!" Katie cried, outraged. "They kill my parents and try to kill this man? This has got to stop."

Harry could say nothing. She was right, but he didn't know how to stop these people. He felt so helpless. He just didn't know what he could do. There were so few of them, and if the mayor and sheriff had taken over the town, Harry was pretty sure they would swell their ranks.

"Come on Boggy, we got a body to bury," Harry said, and headed to the door. He let the dog in, and watched it go to the downed officer. The dog lay down near the man's feet, his large brown eyes looking at the women as they worked on the officer.

Harry stepped out on the porch, where he found a breeze had kicked up. He let it cool his face before turning to Boggy. "Let's go get some water first. I'm thirsty as hell, and it is going to be hot work."

"That's the best thing I've heard all day, I'm near tuckered out from runnin' in them woods. I suspect my heart was near to jumpin' outta my chest," Boggy said, wiping his face with a handkerchief.

Harry laughed and smacked Boggy lightly on his shoulders. He saw movement near the kitchen door and saw Monroe's grinning face. He waved the child back into the house when the boy wanted to follow them. "We gotta do some work, Monroe. Stay in the house, close to your momma," Harry called to the boy. He waited until the child disappeared into the house. He continued walking until he got to the well. He and Boggy took turns drinking from the dipper, the water cold and sweet.

They each collected a shovel from the barn before heading into the woods again. Harry didn't plan on digging a deep grave, but they needed to make sure the animals wouldn't dig the body up either. They would bury the hound with the man and stack some stones on top.

He didn't like having to bury some stranger on his property, but he didn't know what else he could do. They had to be extremely careful now about any kind of diseases. Leaving rotting corpses around was never a good idea.

CHAPTER EIGHTEEN

Katie and Willene worked to strip the unconscious Clay, using scissors to cut away the clothing. Marilyn brought several lanterns and placed them close to the women. She then pulled the curtains away from the window, allowing as much light into the room as possible.

"Marilyn, can you get some of the hot water off the stove please?" Katie asked, her gloved hands moved quickly.

"I sure can. Let me also get Monroe up to his room to play. I don't want him pestering y'all," Marilyn called over her shoulder.

Katie and Willene began to clean the bullet wounds. The one in the abdomen was a through and through and, as far as Katie could tell, nothing vital had been hit, only muscle, no organs, nor major arteries. The one in the shoulder was still in the body. They'd found shotgun pellets peppered on the utility vest. It had taken the brunt of the shot. Overall, Clay had been very, very lucky.

"Let's pack off the wound in his abdomen. We've cleaned it the best we can. We can suture it up after we take care of the shoulder," Katie said, reaching for quick clot and handing it to Willene.

The abdomen dealt with, they turned Clay carefully onto his stomach. Katie then began to wipe at the shoulder. The blood was oozing out and she wiped it clear once more. She then took a syringe filled with saline and flushed the wound. Putting on an LED headlamp, she bent over the wound.

Taking long thin forceps, she blotted the wound and then inserted the instrument into the body as gently as she could. Willene waited, sterile gauze ready to blot the blood away. Katie moved the probe around until she heard the soft clink of metal on metal. She grinned up at Willene. "I think I have it."

Holding her breath, she used the forceps to grab onto the slug. She felt the transmitted vibration of metal forceps hitting the metal of the slug and pulled the small slug out of the body. Blood began to well up and out of the wound and Willene pressed down on the wound with the sterile gauze.

Marilyn returned with a bowl of steaming water. She knelt beside Willene and began to take gauze and clean the officer's back, near his shoulder. Taking the hot water, she rinsed around the wound.

Katie turned back with suture in hand and Willene removed her hand. In short order, the small wound was stitched up. Willene blotted it clean again, wiping away any remaining blood. She then coated it with anti-bacterial ointment.

While Willene was doing that, Katie began to suture the wound on Clay's back, at his waist. Marilyn wiped and kept the area clean. Then the women carefully tipped Clay to his back and Katie began to stitch up the wound on his front.

More anti-bacterial ointment was put on each of the wounds, and then they covered them with sterile gauze and taped it all into place. Marilyn continued to clean Clay up, and tended to his scraped hand. With warm soapy water, she cleaned the worst of it off.

Willene handed her long nose tweezers and Marilyn pulled out several long, thick splinters. Then she put ointment on the palm of his hand and lightly bandaged his hand.

All three women sighed with relief at the same time and began to laugh. They looked at each other sheepishly as they sat around the unconscious Clay.

"Well, I think that went well," Katie said.

Willene and Marilyn grinned and nodded. "Thank God we had the equipment and supplies to help Clay," Willene said, packing up her emergency first aid bag.

"I'd say we are damn lucky to have the supplies. I brought some pain meds and antibiotics with me, but I'll have to wait until Clay wakes so I know he won't have any kind of allergic reaction," Katie said.

She looked down into her bag, reached in and pulled out several vials. "I'm so glad I thought to bring them before I left the ER," she said, looking at Willene.

"That was damn fast thinking, Katie. I'm glad you did. Hopefully we won't have much use for them, but if we need them, I'm glad we've got it," Willene said.

"I'll clean this stuff up," Marilyn said.

"Keep all the used gauze. We can wash and sterilize them. We won't be getting any more of those things," Willene said.

Katie paused, and looked at Willene. "My God, you're right Willene. I'd not even thought of that. I still can't get used to thinking that way."

"Me either," Marilyn admitted.

"I'll help you, Marilyn. We'll get this mess all cleaned up and make Clay as comfortable as we can," Katie said.

Willene went to the linen closet and grabbed a quilt. She laid it over Clay and placed a pillow under his head. Then she lifted his eyelids and checked him.

"Looks like he is doing okay. His respiration looks good and his pulse is good too. He's lucky that his vest caught the brunt of that shot; he could have been so much worse if some of those slugs had got into his lungs," Willene observed.

Katie looked at her hands; they were trembling with spent nerves. She shook her head, thinking it was a miracle indeed. She just hoped he'd not develop an infection. They couldn't do a lot without a proper hospital.

Katie clasped her hands together, trying to stop the tremors. The violence of the last couple of days was overwhelming, and she was having a hard time with it. This poor man had nearly been killed, just for the color of his skin. She knew Clay and knew he was a good man. They'd been friends for years and had even dated a couple times.

Her world was falling apart and once again she didn't know how she was going to cope. Fear was nearly suffocating her; she'd never come up against hate such as this, for her skin color, for her origins.

It was so inconceivable to be hated for something she couldn't help. She'd been raised with love and she had been raised to be color blind. Race had never been a subject in her home; she saw people as either nice or

193

not nice. She'd never judged someone on how they looked, what they believed, or who they loved.

She heard the screen door open and looked up to see Harry come into the house, dirt smeared on his face and arms. She looked around and realized that Marilyn and Willene were gone. She saw his questioning look and smiled, her lips trembling.

"He should be okay. When he wakes, I will see if he has any allergies to antibiotics and pain medication, I brought a few vials of them with me when I left the hospital."

"That's good. Later Boggy and I will put him into the study; I don't think we could get him upstairs," Harry smiled.

"Thanks Harry. I'm going to head back out to the garden to help Willy with the gardening. When he wakes, can you call for me?" Katie asked.

"Sure thing. Is there anything to eat, by the way?" Harry asked, his stomach growling like a berserk gerbil.

Katie laughed. "There is stew in that slow cooker thingy in the kitchen. I'm not sure how done it is, but there is a good chance it is. There are also some biscuits from this morning if you want to eat some of those with it. There is tea on the front porch in a large jar. You'll have to sweeten it."

"Thanks Katie. I'm glad you are here. I'm sure both Earl and Clay will be better for it. I'm not sure what we would have done if you weren't here," Harry said, his eyes warm.

194

"There is no need to thank me. I think this house has become a haven for the unwanted citizens of Beattyville," Katie said sadly. Tears stung the backs of her eyes.

"Well I'm thankful you are here, just the same," Harry said, his smile holding a depth of kindness in it.

Ж

Hobo clasped his stomach; the hunger pangs were excruciating. He and Robby Rob had taken over Mrs. Selma Wise's home two days before, and they'd partied hard. They'd come down hard after running out of anything that could give them a buzz.

Mrs. Wise's body still lay in the kitchen. They had killed her because she didn't have a lot of food in the house. She didn't have much booze either, and Hobo had gone crazy and beaten the old woman. They had drunk what she had and eaten everything they could get their hands on. That morning, they'd looked through the cupboards again, hoping to find anything. They'd managed three cat food cans and a box of prunes.

Mrs. Wise had been thin as a cat whisker, and now Hobo knew why. He had tried to eat the cat food, but retched it up after the first bite. Robby Rob had no such squeamishness and had wolfed down the cans. Feeling like he was going to die, he'd asked Robby Rob to go find him something to eat. That had been some hours ago and Hobo was beginning to worry that Robby Rob wouldn't return.

Getting up from the sofa, he staggered to the door. He had to find either food or drugs. He went out to Earl's truck and climbed in. The keys still in the

195

ignition. He turned the key, and nothing happened. He pumped the gas and tried once more, but nothing happened.

"Christ on a cracker, what the hell is wrong with this damn truck? Piece of shit," Hobo snarled. He slammed the steering wheel with his fist and immediately regretted it. He pulled his fist into his stomach and rocked in pain. Saliva was dripping from his mouth and he bit his lip.

He opened the truck and fell out, landing on all fours. Sluggish, he got up and held onto the truck to steady himself. Black spots began to tap dance before him. Hobo bent over and retched, snot hanging from his nose, his eyes watering. A few minutes later and he stood. Using his arm, he swiped the mess from his face.

Hobo looked around. The street was devoid of people. Cars littered the road, and several dogs sniffed around. His gaze roamed the nearby houses, and he started walking toward the nearest house. He walked up to the door and opened it. He didn't bother to knock or call out, simply walked in. A mother and two small children were startled at his entrance, their faces frozen in shock.

Hobo walked into the kitchen and began opening cabinets. He found a jar of peanut butter. He started jerking open drawers. Finding the silverware, he grabbed a spoon, then commenced shoveling peanut butter into his mouth.

"Michael!" the woman called, fear and alarm lacing her voice.

Hobo ignored her and kept eating and looking through her cabinets. He found a loaf of bread and ripped it open, then smeared the peanut butter on it.

A man came into the kitchen, holding a gun. He raised it. "Get the hell out of my house, mister."

Hobo kept chewing like a dumbstruck cow, and reached out and snatched the gun from the man's outstretched hand. He pointed the gun at the man and shot him in the head. The woman screamed, so Hobo turned and shot her in the head too. The two children, twin boys, stared on in shock. Hobo shot the boys as well.

He turned away and went on looking in the cabinets for more food. Then he went from room to room and found the woman's jewelry box. He pulled out all the trinkets and shoved them into his filthy jean pockets. He went to the bathroom and looked through the medicine cabinet. He couldn't find anything good, and slammed the door so hard the mirror shattered.

He walked back into the kitchen and found the garbage. He emptied out the bag and began filling it with any foodstuff he found in the drawers and cabinets. He pulled out another piece of bread and crammed it in his mouth. He exited the house and ambled back to Mrs. Wise's house.

Ж

Robby Rob walked down Broadway, looking into shop windows. There weren't many people on the street, and the ones that were, watched him. Rob felt the hair standing up on his arm; something about the way they looked at him made his skin crawl. His dark

197

eyes shifted away and eyed a man walking toward him. The man had a smile on his face, but it wasn't a happy smile. It was a nasty smile, a calculating smile.

"Well, hey boy, what y'all doing out wandering around?" the man asked. He had a greasy mullet and a straggly blond beard. He was also missing his front teeth.

"Fuck off, asshole," Robby Rob said, not liking him.

The man's smile evaporated like an ice cube in hell. He pulled out a gun that had been tucked into his pants. "You are under arrest, boy," the man said, a nasty grin beginning to form.

Robby Rob looked the man up and down and laughed. "You ain't no po po."

"I am, boy, and you is under arrest," the man laughed.

"What am I supposed to be arrested for?" Robby Rob asked, not liking the fact that the man kept calling him *boy*.

"You're being arrested for being black, boy," the man said, and barked out a laugh.

"Is you crazy, dude?" Robby Rob laughed, shaking his head.

"Yeah, boy, I am crazy, but you is still under arrest. Now come along with me or I'll shoot your sorry black ass."

EMP ANTEDILUVIAN PURGE   S.A. ISON

CHAPTER NINETEEN

Clay felt hot breath on his face. He opened his eyes. Brian's muzzle was a half inch from his nose. He blinked several times and the dog licked his nose. He jerked his head back and groaned. He looked up as a man appeared from another room. He wondered if the men had caught him. He was lying on the floor and felt vulnerable.

"You're awake. How are you feeling?" the man asked, a kind smile on his face.

Clay looked up at the man. He didn't recognize him, but Brian seemed calm, and Clay knew that if Brian was okay, he was okay. He tried to speak, but his mouth was cotton dry, his tongue sticking to the roof of his mouth. He watched as the man left the room. Beyond the door was a kitchen, and a pitcher stood on the counter. As he watched, the man picked up the pitcher and a glass and came back into the room.

Helping him sit up, the man held the glass and Clay drank greedily from it. He could feel the liquid sliding down his chin and pulled his head back. The man laid him back down.

"My name's Harry Banks. You're in my home. Do you remember what happened to you?" Harry asked as he took a seat on the couch beside him.

"My name is Clay Patterson, and several days ago my cruiser died. So, me and my dog, Brian, had to walk back to town. The thing is, I found quite a few disabled cars. Do you know what is going on?" Clay asked, sure he wasn't going to like the answer.

199

"I'll fill you in after you tell me what happened," Harry said kindly.

"Sure. Anyway, we had to stay at some old guy's home the first night, real nice fella. So, me and Brian kept walking and we slept in the woods, and then kept walking. Christ, my feet were killing me. Pops, the old guy, gave me sports shoes, but they only helped a little," Clay's voice was beginning to get scratchy.

Harry grabbed the glass of water and helped Clay up to drink again. Clay thanked Harry, and was laid back down. "So, while walking, I'd not seen anyone, I mean anyone in a car. Then this truck drives up and a bunch of rednecks were in it. I asked them if I could have a ride. The guy had a shotgun and looked like he really wanted to kill me." He wiped his mouth with his uninjured arm.

"They did want to kill you, trust me," Harry said, his hands hanging limply between his knees. "We believe that a widespread solar flare hit Earth five days ago, causing what we believe to have been an EMP. It has knocked all electrical components out; we think the whole of the U.S., and perhaps the world."

"Oh, my sweet baby Jesus, are you sure?" Clay asked. He felt as though someone had hit him in the gut.

"As sure as we can be. Everything, our smart phones, cars, electrical grids, at least locally, is down. We've not seen nor heard any airplanes flying over. Being in the mountains, we are cut off. But as far as we know, we are down hard," Harry said.

"Yeah, I can believe it. I felt like the only man on Earth while out there," Clay said, a small tremor of remembrance running through him.

Harry pressed on. "Apparently, Sheriff Yates and Mayor Audrey have taken over Beattyville and turned it into a KKK haven. Looks like they are killing all non-whites," Harry explained, his multicolored eyes glaring. "Those men shot you because you're black. Apparently, they felt free enough to chase you down. Unfortunately for them, they chased you onto my property, and your dog led us to you. You're lucky he was with you. I shot one of the men. Looks like they are part of or affiliated with the KKK. There are several other people living here; you may know them. I grew up here, but I've been away the last few years, serving in the Army."

Clay was stunned. He didn't know what to say. He wasn't very surprised to hear about the sheriff and the mayor; their barely concealed contempt for people of any color, and their off-color jokes, had made it clear what they thought. But the power down forever? It was all making sense, given all the abandoned vehicles and lack of people.

"How long will the power be off, do you think?" Clay asked. He already knew the answer, but really wanted to hear something different.

"It may well never come back, Clay, at least not here in the remote mountains. Maybe in larger cities they may get it back, but that won't be for years. And I'm fairly certain the cities are in ruins by now, with deaths aplenty. We discussed it here a few days ago.

201

No electricity means no water for most, and no food," Harry said, shrugging.

"I have a lot of food at home. If we could get there, we could bring it here," Clay offered.

"Thanks. If we can get to your house, we will look. For now, though, I think it is best we stay put, at least until you are up to showing us the way. But know that people are going to be out scavenging for food and may well have found your supplies. There may be nothing left, as it has been five days," Harry said.

"Damn it. I can't believe this is happening. What the hell am I going to do?" Clay asked, his voice trembling, strain causing his voice to crack.

"Don't worry, Clay. This is your home now. We have enough food for all of us, and I think we will need your help and expertise to help keep us all alive," Harry said, a warm smile on his face.

"Thank you, Harry, thank you. I remember you now, from high school. I was a freshman and you and your sister, Willene, were seniors. You've changed a lot, grown up." Clay smiled, then gritted his teeth against a flare up of pain.

"Are you in any pain, Clay?" Harry asked, his heavy brows drawing together.

"Yeah, I am," Clay said, suddenly feeling weak and tired.

"I'll get Katie and let her know. She said she has some pain meds," Harry said, standing up.

"Katie's here?" Clay asked, trying to sit up, then groaned and lay back down.

"Yes. Someone was trying to kill her as well. They killed her parents, the cowardly bastards," Harry said, fury flushing his face red.

"Lord have mercy. What is this world coming to?" Clay said, feeling the breath knocked out of him once again.

"I'd say it's going to hell in a handbasket. I'll go get Katie."

Clay lay back, his hand absently stroking Brian's head. It was so much to take in, and so unbelievable. His heart broke for Katie. He'd known her parents. They'd been wonderful people and he knew Katie had been close to them.

He looked around the room. All the windows were open and a breeze was blowing in. He could see out the screen door onto a porch. He looked back into the kitchen. It was a tidy home, and big. It was now his home, and Clay knew he was damn lucky to be there, and to be alive.

Katie watched, fascinated, as Willene and Marilyn filled a large metal tub with hot water. Two large metal tubs sat on lumber racks. The small metal handles of the tubs had larger wooden handles attached to them, and could be levered to tip the dirty water out onto the ground below. Below the tubs was a gravel bed that covered the area, ensuring the ground didn't get too muddy. The tubs were roughly waist high, about three feet.

She'd been told that Boggy had built them a makeshift laundry out by the clotheslines. He had also built a fire pit, so the water could easily be heated and dumped directly into the tubs.

"That is a nice little operation you have here," Katie said, taking note of the stacked cinderblocks and heavy grate that sat on top. There was a fire burning below, and a stack of firewood nearby, with buckets of cold water waiting to be heated.

"Boggy was such a sweetie for setting this up for me," Willene said. "I told him we needed to set something up to wash clothes. I wanted to put heated water into the large tub, but I needed something to heat the water with. What is really nice is each tub can be used to wash, rinse or soak clothing, whatever you need to do."

"That really makes it handy, to boil or heat water outside, and that large pot can hold quite a bit of water," Katie said, admiring the set up.

"It's an old canning pot, and when I can find another one, we can have two pots boiling hot water. For now, this will work," Willene said.

"What is the mop bucket for?" Katie asked, looking at the large yellow mop bucket; she'd seen them at the hospital. It had the mop squeezing bracket mounted to the bucket.

"That is the rinse water. Once you wash your clothes, you rinse in that large bucket. Then you put the clothing into the mop squeezer and squeeze the water out, instead of trying to wring it out," Marilyn said smiling widely.

"Oh, that is smart!" Katie laughed, delighted. She'd hand-washed things in the past, and it was always a pain to wring them out.

"Yeah, and then you just hang them on the line," Willene said, laughing as she indicated the clotheslines like Vanna White, eliciting laughter from the women.

"I figure we can choose a day to wash our stuff, with each of us responsible for our own laundry. But, using the large tub, we can get it done at once or when we find time," Willene said.

"That's good. I don't think I want to wash Boggy or Earl's clothes." Marilyn made a face, and all the women busted out laughing, their hilarity filling the air.

Katie looked around and saw Boggy's head peeking around the corner of the house. And then she saw Harry looking through the kitchen door, apparently drawn to their laughter. They all laughed harder when they saw the men, and when the men quickly disappeared, the women laughed all the harder, nearing hysterical. They were all bent at the waist, wiping tears from their eyes. Katie almost fell to the ground, her knees going weak with hilarity.

"I imagine they thought we were laughing about them," Willene said, still laughing and wiping the tears from her eyes.

"We were," Marilyn said, and doubled over into another fit of laughing. That made the women laugh more, and Monroe came around the house, a large grin on his face. The women began to calm down, wiping the tears away, and periodic giggling burst out before they got themselves under control.

205

"Lord, that felt good," Katie said, using the edge of her shirt to wipe her eyes and nose.

"It sure was, but I mean it. I don't want to wash those men's clothes. I've got enough with mine and Monroe's," Marilyn said, and the women began to vibrate once more with suppressed hilarity.

"Whas so funny, Mommy?" Monroe asked his mother, his arms wrapped around her hips.

Katie watched with a soft smile as Marilyn bent and kissed her son, then gave him a shirt. "Nothing, honey, but it is time for you to learn how to wash your own clothes," Marilyn said, a broad smile on her face.

The kitchen screen door opened and Harry stood at the door, smiling. He waved Katie over to him. Katie smiled at the women and then walked across the yard to the house. When she got there, Harry was standing in the kitchen, drinking coffee.

"Clay is awake and in some pain. I figured you could go see him," Harry said, a question lurking in the depths of his eyes.

Katie grinned. She knew he wanted to know what the women had been laughing at, but she wouldn't tell. She had to bite the inside of her cheek to keep from busting out laughing again. She sighed heavily. "Thanks. I'll go see to him."

Ж

Mary Deets woke up, her body hurting. She didn't know if it were day or night, or how long she'd been in this hole. She could hear others moving around, and someone was asleep beside her, the heat radiating from the body. She wasn't sure who it was, as people took turns sleeping beside her.

The people down here in the coal mine had made a comfortable pallet for her and given her extra food and water. They were very protective of her, as she was five months pregnant. Which was more than could be said for those two officers and their lackeys, who had handled her roughly.

Gideon Elliot, her neighbor, had come over when he'd heard her screams. Officers Gene Grady and Tom Learn had at least had the decency to look ashamed when they'd come to her door. There'd been two other men with them she didn't know. One of them had handled her roughly, pulling her out of her home.

She had screamed for Howard, her husband. Grady had shocked her to her core when he laughed and said Howard was all over the office.

Mary didn't know a lot of what had happened after that; she'd gone numb and buckled in their arms. She remembered Gideon coming out his door, screaming at the officers. They'd beaten Gideon and thrown him into the back of a truck, then dragged his wife and two teen sons in after him, their hands zip tied. Gideon's wife, Julie, had held her in her arms as the truck bounced around enroute to the coal mine.

There'd been a line of people, many of them black, some white, and a couple Hispanics. Around them were white men, lots of white men, many sporting swastika tattoos. They all had weapons. The women in the line were crying, holding their children closely. She was dragged roughly out of the truck and once more Gideon protested her rough handling. He was beaten to the ground, and Julie had cried out. The men had shoved her and her children to the line along with Mary.

Mary had been terrified when she was lowered into the depths of the coal mine with Julie, Gideon, and their boys. There were no lights, and her heart had slammed hard into her chest. She could barely breathe, and her hands cradled her belly protectively, her body vibrating. Julie's arms were around her and her boys, Boyd and Steven.

Mary had felt the damp cool air around her and the oily smell of coal. The light from above had faded, and then it was gone. She had no idea how long they'd been down in this hole.

Mary sat up slowly, feeling her way around. There was a dim light about fifteen feet away, and she carefully felt her way up and away from the sleeping person. She made her way carefully to the candlelight. Someone took her arm gently and led her the rest of the way.

"Good morning, Mary. How are you feeling?" It was Gideon guiding her.

"I'm okay. I dreamed of Howard. What's going on?" Mary asked, her voice trembling with the dream and remembered reality.

"We're getting ready to go to work," Gideon said. "They sent down more food, and I want you to eat. We asked for dust masks for folks down here." He pressed one into her hands as he spoke. "I want you to wear it at all times. This coal dust is not good for you or the baby." His face was pale in the candlelight, though

208

black streaks of coal dust were all over his face. Beneath the streaks, she saw that his bruises were healing. He and his wife were older, and had always been good neighbors. Julie had been excited about Mary's pregnancy.

They'd managed to work out that anyone who tried to protect or harbor blacks, Hispanics, Asians, and non-Christians would end up in the mines, working. They'd been told that the KKK ruled now, and that if they wanted to eat, to live, then they'd have to work in the coal mines. If they refused, they'd be left in the dark to starve to death. Mary didn't know how many people were down here, but most were black, like her.

There were quite a few white people, but it was getting harder to tell they were white, as the coal dust covered everyone and everything. They kept the food covered with heavy cloths. Mary could feel the grit in every crack and crevasse. Some of the people had given her extra clothing to keep her warm and dry.

Gideon handed her a large chunk of bread and a bottle of water.

"I hate to ask, but is there any way they can send milk down for me and the children? My baby needs it, and I know the children do as well."

"I'll ask. I'm seeing about getting more blankets and fruits and vegetables as well, and some candles. If those idiots want us to work, then they will need to keep us strong. I'm getting ready to go down into the shafts. Is there anything else I can get you?" Gideon asked.

"No, I'm fine. Where is Julie?" Mary asked.

"She is with the boys. They are searching some of the tunnels near us, looking for things we can use. We are thinking of a way to get word out that we are here, and hopefully someone will help us," Gideon assured her.

He patted her arm and turned to go toward the back of the tunnel with the other men and the older boys. Each put a hard hat on with a headlamp. They all carried pickaxes, shovels and buckets.

Mary watched the men go, still nibbling on the bread. At least it was good. She hoped the KKK didn't put poison in their food. Her heart hurt, thinking of her husband being betrayed by his fellow officers. Tears fell silently down her cheeks. She didn't wipe them away, as they would only mix with the coal dust. She then took the dust mask and placed it over her nose and mouth. She felt as though she couldn't breathe, but she knew it was all in her mind. She moved slowly back to her sleeping pallet, trying not to bump into the walls and low ceilings.

She dreaded when she had to go to the bathroom: it was terrible trying to clean herself in the dark and with the grit all over her. The smell was also hellish after all these people had used the three buckets. She knew it was unhealthy and it frightened her. Her baby was now her only connection to Howard. She'd heard from several people that her home and Gideon and Julie's home had been burnt to the ground.

She turned her head toward the candle; someone was being lowered down. A man was cursing loudly, the foul language echoing down the tunnels. A new

EMP ANTEDILUVIAN PURGE   S.A. ISON

arrival. Mary turned and lay back down on her pallet. There was nothing for her to do, and the less energy she used, the more the calories she had consumed went to her baby. She could feel the tears sliding down the corner of her eyes to her cheeks. Her heart was broken, shattered with the knowledge of her lost husband. How had things gone so bad, so quickly? She wiped at her face and felt the grit and stopped. All she could do now was think of the unborn child and his lost father. She needed to focus and keep their baby safe. She needed to stay alive. Her hand went down to her stomach and she felt movement. Her heart bumped with joy and sorrow.

CHAPTER TWENTY

Earl held onto the stair railing as he came down from his bedroom. The aroma of coffee had snaked up to his room. He was feeling halfway human, finally out of the brain-numbing pain. Boggy told him Clay was at the house, and that he'd been shot by a bunch of white boys, probably KKK.

Earl strode into the living room, and found Clay sleeping on the couch, a dog asleep on the floor beside him. The creak from the old floor caused Clay's eyes to pop open.

"Sorry I woke ya, Clay," Earl said, ducking his head.

"Hey Earl, you look like crap," Clay said laughing, then winced.

Earl sniggered and went to the armchair nearest the couch and sat down. He leaned over and shook Clay's outstretched hand. Marilyn came into the living room carrying two cups of coffee. She smiled at the men and handed each a coffee.

"How are you feeling, boys?"

"Fine," they said in unison, then grinned at each other.

Katie came down the stairs and joined them. She smiled at Clay, and he sat up a little straighter. Earl raised an eyebrow, curious. Harry came in from outside, the screen door slamming behind him. He and Clay nodded to Harry, and Earl sipped his coffee.

"I wanted to have a meeting with everyone, if y'all are feeling up to it," Harry said to Clay and Earl.

212

Both men nodded, and Harry headed into the kitchen. He returned with a cup of coffee and egg biscuit with ham. Willene also came in, carrying a whole plate filled with the fluffy biscuits.

His stomach growled loudly and he looked around sheepishly. It had been a while since he'd eaten regular food; Willene had been feeding him a lot of oatmeal and soft egg and gravy.

Years ago, with the mining accident, he'd not only lost his lower leg but also six of his front teeth. Hobo's beating had knocked out more teeth. He had most of his molars, but all his front teeth were now gone. His mouth was still sore, and Marilyn and Willene had insisted he rinse his mouth out several times a day with warm salt water. They didn't want him to develop an infection in his jaw. So far, he'd healed well.

The over-the-counter pain meds Marilyn had given him had helped, and he was able to eat with relatively little pain now. Clay's dog was whining, and Harry walked over to let the dog out to join Charley. Earl heard the dogs barking at each other; at least they sounded friendly. He sipped his coffee and nibbled on the delicious buttery biscuit. It was nirvana, and he was starting to feel whole once more.

"It seems that the mayor is purging the town with extreme prejudice," Harry began, all faces on him.

Earl thought he looked a little tired, and was determined to stand his watch tonight. "You done said a mouthful, brother. I reckon that peckerwood mayor will be livin' high on the hog now," Earl said, noticing Harry's lip twitch with humor.

"Yes, and for now, I'm sorry to say, there isn't much we can do about it. When you're up to it in a day or two, Earl, I want to go out on reconnaissance. When Clay is better, we need to figure out how to even the playing field," Harry said and took a bite of his biscuit.

"That's going to be hard to do," Clay said. "The good folks of Beattyville are spread out in the hills and mountains. Many may not even know what is going on. I sure didn't until you told me. We are now in a new era of isolation, like our ancestors. Kentucky, and especially the people of the mountains, have historically lived isolated. The mountains are a great separator."

"He's right," Katie said. "How can we determine who is with the mayor and the sheriff and who is not? Unless these people are running around in bedsheets. We can't assume every white person is with him."

Earl saw Boggy flinch. He was quiet. He knew the young man was afraid. Hell, he was afraid. He'd heard many of his friends talk trash about others of different colors, but he'd never bought into it himself. He had always kept his opinion to himself.

"I agree," Willene said. "How will we know who we can trust? And how can we help those in town, and anyone in the mountains, in danger of the mayor's ignorance and evil?"

"That's going to be hard, and honestly, I really don't know right now. We'll need help. maybe Alan could get in contact with people who would be willing to help us. I hate to say, but we may not have the capacity to help anyone but ourselves. We do have in

214

our favor the fact that we are isolated and therefore not open to a lot of attack. I hope," Harry said. "I know we are a few days to a week's walk from Lexington, and I imagine they are imploding by now. I don't know if we will see anyone soon."

"Whoever we do see will be looking to take what we have, don't you think?" Marilyn asked.

"I'd say yes, and we may end up having to fight them. We just don't have the resources. And to invite total strangers into our home may end up bringing danger here," Harry said.

Earl listened, his heart sinking. He knew his friends were right. Whoever came here wasn't coming to be friendly and to help them; they were going to be coming to help themselves. He couldn't blame them, but this was his home now and his people, and he needed to help defend the house and his friends.

"I walked for near on twelve hours a day and I was half way here when my car stopped running," Clay said, his dark brows drawn together, "it was a hard trek. As the crow flies, it isn't that long a distance, but coming along all the winding mountain roads, it takes one hell of a long time. I am afraid that anyone along that way will be hit. If they don't have weapons to protect themselves and their homes, they will be casualties."

"If they're starving, I'd expect many will be tuckered out and be plum tired before they get here," Boggy said shyly, clutching his coffee cup to his chest.

"True, but if they have transportation or steal it, they can be here quick," Harry cautioned. "We have a high vantage point here and can see what is coming down the road. If they are on foot and walking the woods, I'm hoping the dogs will alert us, as well as our warning traps."

"Gimme another day, I think I'll be better. Right now, I'm just a little stove up for the moment," Earl said apologetically. He wished he could help them more now.

"There is no big rush. You just heal, Earl," Harry said, smiling.

Earl relaxed back in his chair as he listened to everyone discuss strategies. He still could not get over the fact that the sheriff and mayor had out and out murdered people because of their color. People he'd known all his life, families that had lived in these mountains for generations. Boggy's granny had been a sweet and loving woman and he'd eaten many times at her table. To think that Audrey would have tried to kill her, and would try to kill Boggy, was beyond him; these were good people.

He'd known Clay all his life, remembered him from when he had been a senior in high school and the tall string bean Clay had been as a freshman, awkward and goofy. How could these people want to kill a good man? And Dr. Katie? How could they want her dead? She was kind and had always treated him with compassion, especially when he'd been injured. He'd been a little in love with her himself. He could feel a blush creeping up his face and quickly brought the coffee cup up to hide his discomfiture.

He really didn't know what they could do. Getting rid of the KKK felt like an overwhelming task to him. Earl didn't think he was a coward, but he was no Hieronymus Banks either. To him, Harry was larger than life. He wondered once more what his life would have been like if he'd followed Harry into the army.

Ж

As Alan Tate walked along Beattyville Road, which was near the center of town, he saw an old couple shuffling along. Their skin hung on them liked they were walking raisins, blue veins roped their hands, and their knobby bones were sharp. He nodded politely to them. They stopped him.

"Son, you got any food on you? We're plum outta food," the old man said, his old voice wavering. His old eyes looked faded like dead leaves.

"No sir, but I heard maybe that mayor has some. He got them stores safe, an' I reckon they'd given totes of grub an' water," Alan told him.

Both old people made faces of sour disappointment, their lips wrinkling alarmingly. The old woman harrumphed. "That obnoxious fat man, that gluttonous bastard? Giving food away? I'll believe it when I see it."

"Thank you, son," the old man said, reaching up and patting his ropey hand on Alan's shoulder.

Alan watched as the old couple walked away, their slow shuffling movements painful to watch. He wondered if they would survive, and sorrow struck his young heart.

217

He knew he could keep himself and his grandpa fed, he could shoot really good and there were plenty of boomers, such as red squirrels, rabbits, and other varmints. Alan also knew plenty of wild plants to eat. There wouldn't be a lot, but they could survive. There was also the Lee's garden; he'd helped them plant it and tend it. Their house had been destroyed, but their garden had been left alone.

He noticed a poster tacked to a post. He walked up to it and read it. The blood drained from his face. Looking around, he yanked the paper off the post and walked away quickly. He needed to get to Harry's quick and show this to him.

When he reached his home twenty minutes later, he went in to see his grandpa. The old man was sitting in front of an old box television set, smoking a Camel cigarette.

Alan walked over and kissed the top of his white fuzzy head. "I'm headin' out, Pop Pop. Can I get you anything before I go?" Alan asked.

"Naw, son. I'll stay right on here and smoke my cigs. Ain't nothin' on the boob tube," he grumbled.

Alan shook his head and went to the kitchen and opened a box of peanut butter crackers. He put a few on a plate and got his grandpa a soda pop. He placed the plate and drink on the coffee table. He kissed his grandfather once more on the top of his head and left the old man.

The truck rattled down the road. Alan knew this would more than likely be his last trip out unless he could find more gas. He was sorry. He liked Dr. Katie,

218

Earl, and Willene. He didn't know the others very well, but they all seemed nice. He knew he was just a kid, but he'd felt important when he'd saved the doctor. It seemed so unreal that people would want to kill her. He'd known her most of his life. Her folks had also been nice, always giving him homemade cookies.

He bit down on his lip, his eyes tearing up thinking about her parents and the way those men had treated them and then killed them. His face contorted in a rictus of sorrow and he swallowed hard. He'd never seen that kind of hate or violence. He'd only seen stuff on television and movies, and reality just wasn't the same. His heart slammed hard against his thin chest.

The Lee's had never said a bad thing about anyone, they'd never hurt anyone. Dr. Katie was so wonderful, and he knew he was half in love with her. How could he not be? She was beautiful and sweet and so kind. Those men would have hurt her like they hurt her momma. He'd not told her that those men had raped her mother. He could not bring himself to tell her. And those bad men had killed two men in the street, just for trying to help. He just didn't understand any of this.

He coughed out a hard cry and wiped his nose with his shirtsleeve. Those men had laughed all the while, and had made Mr. Lee watch. Then they'd killed both of them. They had then stood over the bodies and laughed and kicked at them. It wasn't enough for them to hurt them and kill them, they had to kick their dead bodies as well. Finally, the men had tired of the fun and gone into the house.

He'd felt so helpless and he'd wanted to help the Lee's, but his grandpa said those men would kill him and laugh the whole time. There was nothing he could do but go get Dr. Katie. He waited, watching the house, dancing back and forth on his feet. He'd wanted to leave then and there, but his grandfather told him to wait until the men left. They'd more than likely take their truck if he tried to leave while they were tearing up the Lee's home.

It had seemed like a long time. He'd watched as the men went in and out of the house, taking bags of food and items from the house, laughing all the time. Several times, they had walked by the bodies and kicked them. He could only stand there and watch, and cry. His heart had broken over and over as each kick connected with the bodies.

He couldn't understand that kind of hate, that kind of abuse. What kind of men were they? How could they do this with such joy? He wondered, if they had children, what kind of fathers were they? Did they teach their children to hate? His grandpa had always been a hard man, but a good man. He'd never said a bad or unkind word about anyone.

His grandpa had stood with him at the window. He'd been crying as well, and kept his old hand on Alan's shoulder, whether to hold him there or to hold himself up, Alan didn't know. He'd rarely seen his grandfather weep, and it broke his heart even more to see his strong grandpa cry.

Alan shook the morbid memories away. He had to pay attention, as the curves around the mountain were treacherous. He slowed the truck and then sped up, weaving in and around abandoned cars. His mind soon wandered back to Dr. Katie and her family.

He enjoyed helping Dr. Katie's father in the back yard, in the garden. He'd buried the couple, his grandpa helping as much as he could. His grandpa was fragile, and the sorrow had taken its toll. He had cried the whole time while he buried them. Hate was a concept that was so alien to him. In his sixteen years, he'd always been loved.

Coming up on a hairpin turn, he slowed the truck down. Then slammed the brakes. He pulled his truck off the road and stumbled out, falling to the ground. Tears began to stream down his face once more. Then he stood, walked a step or two, then fell back to his knees, oblivious to the rocks cutting through his skin. Alan began to retch, his stomach heaving violently.

CHAPTER TWENTY-ONE

Before him was a family, Puerto Rican, hanging from a large oak tree. He barely recognized Robert, his friend from school, who was a year younger.

The boy's face was nearly black and bloated, as were those of his mother and father, their eyes bulging obscenely. Bloated flies landed on their faces, going in and out of their opened mouths. Alan vomited again, heavy saliva hanging from his open mouth.

Though he could see the sight, he couldn't comprehend it. They'd been hung. His breath, coming in harsh cries, tore out of his chest. Then he spotted a piece of paper pinned to the woman's dress. He crawled toward them, his knees scraping along the asphalt of the road, until he came to the side of the road. He tottered violently as he stood, his legs weak and unsteady.

His hand shook as he snatched the paper off. He choked and cried out as his hand gently touched one of Robert's sneakers, causing the body to swing. He fell to his knees once more. He wiped his arm across his face, trying to tamp the sobs down as well as the urge to retch. He didn't want anyone to hear him. He opened his mouth, bit down on his forearm, and screamed into it, low and guttural. He bent at the waist and screamed over and over.

Then he heard something. The sound hadn't come from him, and neither was it the birds in the trees or the insect life. His head jerked sideways and he froze, listening intently. There it was again, not too far away.

222

He stood on wobbly legs and walked toward the noise. His hand clamped hard across his mouth when he looked into the bushes. There was Robert's baby sister, Angela, the fourteen-month-old, still secure in her car seat. Her large brown eyes had tears standing in them and her thumb was stuck in her small mouth. His own eyes teared up once more and he leaned over and picked up the car seat. It was heavy, but he lifted it over the bush.

Running back to his truck, he blocked Angela's view of her family. He secured the seat in the truck and got back in. He looked back once more at his friend, and swallowed the cry that wriggled its way up his throat. He needed to get the baby to safety, and he knew that Dr. Katie would know what to do.

Ж

Wilber Tate watched his grandson speed away in the truck. Something had gotten into that boy. All this grim business. He looked over to the Lee's burned-out home and shook his head. He'd asked Alan what had happened to Dr. Katie, but his grandson had said she hadn't been at the hospital. Wilber sure hoped she was someplace safe.

Anger surged once more. His friend and neighbor, Chul Lee, murdered by merciless cowards, and his lovely wife, Nari, raped and murdered. And then both of their bodies had been abused. What kind of animals did that? The two men who'd tried to help had been gunned down before they even got across the street. He'd had to hold on to his grandson, who'd have gone out to try to help their friends and just got himself killed.

Wilber Tate wasn't a coward. He'd make sure to get those men, but he knew he had to do it smart. The day after the Lee's had been murdered, he and Alan had buried them. Then he'd gone to see his friends, men he knew he could trust. He'd been in the Army years ago, during the Vietnam conflict. Wilber laughed, it was a goddamn war, not a conflict. And now they were facing a war in their own town.

He'd first gone to Bonaparte Patterson, or Boney, a fellow Vietnam vet. Boney had a sixth cousin who was black and also worked on the police force. He'd figured his friend would know if his cousin was alive or not. Boney had been a sniper, and though the man was near eighty, Boney still had the sharp eyes of the killer he'd been long ago. Wilber was also a good shot.

Boney also had kinfolk all around Beattyville and in the surrounding mountains. They were a fractious group, but none would stand for the KKK taking out one of their own. They were very clannish that way. He would go to Boney now and see what could be done. They'd been meeting in secret with all the hell that was breaking loose.

Wilber locked the house and walked by the Lee home, his heart filled yet again with anger and sorrow. He scrubbed his hand over his unshaven face, making a rasping noise, as though trying to rub the sorrow away. He knew nothing could. He and Boney were getting organized; they were starting to work on a plan, a plan that would end the KKK's hold over Beattyville and bring about its destruction. When he'd gone to Boney the day after the assault on the Lee's, they'd talked about what the future held for them and their families.

"It's only gonna get worse, Wil, you know that," Boney had said.

"Sure do. When them coward dogs come and did that to them fine folks, I knew the world was going straight to hell," Wilber said, a sour taste in his mouth.

"Yep. They're a bunch of sorry broke dick dogs, the lot of em," Boney had said and spat tobacco juice off the porch.

Ralph Edison and his twin Abram were seventy-seven; they had also been there at the first meeting. They were both old Army men as well. Sherman Collins, who'd been in the Navy, no accounting for taste, was seventy-four, and Hoover Neil, a retired postmaster, who was seventy-nine. The youngest member of their group was Thornton Sherman, an ex-Marine who was seventy.

The men had talked about what supplies they had, though all had good stockpiles of food and supplies. Thornton was the only one who still had a wife, all the other men were either widowers or divorced. Living in a coal town was a hard life, and especially hard on the families who worked in the mines. They'd all spent time in the coal mines. There just wasn't much work.

Wilber stopped and looked around and listened. The air was still and no sounds. It was still something to get used to. He was closer to town; he and most of his friends lived on the outskirts of town, on bigger properties that were not so close to neighbors. A man

225

was sitting on his porch with a shotgun across his lap. He nodded to Wilber and he lifted a hand in greeting.

"Howdy. How's it goin'?" Wilber called, lifting a weathered hand.

"Not sa good, had some real peckerwood boys to come around wantin' supplies for the town. Said the mayor wants a little from folks," the man said, and spat a stream of dark liquid off the side of the porch.

"Well that don't sound right. What is you supposed to do for your family?" Wilber asked.

"Don't rightly think the mayor gives a good damn. Told them peckerwood boys ta move along, me and my Betsy." The man gave a grin and held up the shotgun.

Wilber grinned back. "Good man. Gotta protect your family first." He lifted a hand in farewell and kept walking.

Most of his supplies and food were hidden in the basement. Years ago, he'd seen the devastation and rampant poverty in Vietnam, people starving to death while armies and governments flourished. He himself had grown up in poverty, but not near as bad as what he'd seen in that faraway place.

He'd vowed then that he'd not ever let his family go hungry. His good wife and his daughter had canned food from the garden, and also meat from hunting. He was especially fond of venison after it had been canned for a couple years. It was tender, and he ate it over rice.

Wilber laughed to himself as his stomach rumbled. He'd built a hidden room in the basement that was covered with a large floor-to-ceiling shelf. He'd attached several large hinges to the shelf, allowing him to swing the shelf open to access the hidden room, where he kept most of the jarred foodstuffs.

He also kept boxes of instant rice, potatoes, and dried beans. It was dark and cool in the room, keeping the food supply hidden and well preserved. He'd eaten from jars that had been well over ten years old, and the food tasted near fresh and delicious.

Wilber arrived at Boney's house, situated on a low hill surrounded by large overgrown rose bushes. Boney was up on the porch, smoking a pipe. He lifted a hand in greeting. Wilber could smell the scent of roses mixed with the fragrant smoke.

It was an hour walk or better, but Wilber didn't mind. He'd had his back broken years ago at the coal mine. Dr. Katie had seen him in the yard one day, barely able to move. She'd insisted he be checked out. When she'd asked him what activity he did on a daily basis, he'd said armchair jockey.

They'd both had a good laugh, then she told him that in another few years he'd be stuck in that chair if he didn't get out and walk and move about. Since that day, he had taken long walks, sometimes up to four hours. His back felt a whole lot better and he slept better at night. He once more hoped Dr. Katie was alive and doing okay.

His knees creaked as he climbed the steps and came onto the broad porch that surrounded the home. He took a rocking chair near Boney, then took out his pipe and tamped in fresh tobacco. He lit it and drew the smoke into his mouth. He never fully inhaled; some folks did, he didn't. After working in the coal mines, it was hard to breathe sometimes.

"Feller down the road told me mayor's now trying to take food and guns," Wilber said without preamble.

"Yep. Them peckerwoods stopped by here. Told them ta have a look and welcome to what they could find."

Wilber snorted and wheezed laughter, causing smoke to escape from his nostrils. He wiped at them absently. "They find much?" Wilber asked, already knowing the answer.

"Naw, just a half poke of flour and sugar in the bowl. A can or two of beans an' some eggs," Boney said, laughing. "They come out lookin' at me, asked was that all I had. Said it was and did *they* have anything to spare?" Boney laughed harder.

Wilber joined in the laughter. Boney was a small wizened man, not much to look at, but was sharper than a well-honed scythe. When he got home, he'd clear out more food and put it in the basement, hiding it behind the swinging shelving. He'd also put his long rifles down there, as well and his ammo.

"They asked about any guns, said I had a broke down shot gun." Boney gave a gummy grin. "They left upset; guess they found the rotten tatters I'd left'em." Boney barked out laughter and slapped his knee, and rocked back and forth with glee.

Wilber shook his head, grinning. Boney loved his fun, tormenting peckerwoods. He drew in his pipe and let the smoke pearl out from his mouth. "Any word from your young'un, cousin Clay?"

Boney raised a brow and looked sideways at Wilber. His mouth turned down and shook his head. "Ain't heard nothin'. Got my feeler's out. Expect I'll hear something at some time," Boney said.

"We need to do something about them cowards, Boney. I suspect they're gonna make our lives intolerable," Wilber said, relaxing his body into the rocker. There was a breeze blowing, and with it the perfume of roses and lilies cooled his heated skin. He could hear some jays bickering in the back of the house, more than likely pestering a cat.

"Yep, we sure do. What you figger we could do, Wil?"

"Well, I expect you're a sharp shooter, and I ain't so bad neither. Mayhap we start pickin' them little pissants off, one at a time. Say at night, or from a good hiding place," Wilber suggested.

"Young man, that is a fine idea. All our boys are good shots, even that Navy puke, Sherman," he said and laughed.

Wilber grinned and rocked a bit more. "You heard about all them folks that's getting put in the coal mine?" Wilber asked. He drew on his pipe a little harder, the bowl, the tinder trying to go out.

"Yep. Them craven bastards is puttin' women an' young'uns down there. We gotta do something about that too," Boney said.

Both men sat in silence, each in their own deep thoughts. It would take planning and daring. They'd need more help than just the seven of them. They'd need to recruit. It was a tricky thing, a balancing act;

you never knew where some folk's loyalties lay. Any of them could end up in the mine along with the rest of those poor folks.

Ж

Hobo awoke in a pool of cold congealed vomit, his head thundering. The smell of the vomit made his stomach heave and roil, and he swallowed back the ropy saliva that was hanging out of his mouth. He could feel the cold wet vomit clinging to the side of his head and shoulder. He kept heaving and sat up, his hand blindly feeling around for a bottle of water or something. His eyes felt as though sand and glass had been ground in.

Hobo knew he needed to eat, and he needed drugs or booze. He'd eaten everything he'd stolen from the house next door, but it hadn't been enough. It was time to go looking again. He pulled himself up and groaned heavily, sweat popping out on his forehead and on his chin beneath his dirty beard, mixing with the dried vomit.

He reached the door and was glad for small mercies; it was dusk. Stumbling out of the house, he walked over to the truck and then remembered it didn't run anymore. Cursing under his breath, he turned and began walking unsteadily up the street. He scrutinized houses for potential targets. He saw faces in some, men, and so he kept walking. He needed a weak target.

He stopped for a moment feeling dizzy, the nausea rising once more. He bent at the waist, placing the palms of his hands on his knees. He spat a glob of foulness onto the ground. Standing, he proceeded on down the road.

Finally, he found a home that had potential. Ugly lawn ornaments littered the ground, and many old people he knew liked those wretched things.

Smiling, he walked up to the house and opened the door and walked in. He looked around and saw a bent, wizened old woman who resembled one of the rotund little gnomes, down to the red rosy cheeks. She looked up. A smile trembled on her wrinkled face, her old faded eyes watery and unfocused. She was standing at a large table on which several bright solar lanterns stood, illuminating the room.

Hobo walked over to the old woman and hit her with a closed fist, knocking her to the ground. She lay, unmoving, on the ground. She was still alive, he could see, but essentially out of the way, blood gushing from her nose and mouth. He walked over and squatted near her. Poking at her gray head, he heard her moan. He stood and stepped away, and slipped. Blood on the bottom of his shoe. He looked around the living and dining room.

Up atop a large oak buffet and hutch were stacked various boxes and bags. Behind the clutter was a bottle. It looked like a bottle of Jack Daniels, and his mouth watered. Just what he needed. He drew the back of his wrist across his mouth, vomit smearing across his face.

His head was throbbing and his stomach still roiling. He pulled an oak chair over and climbed up. With one hand holding onto the back of the chair, Hobo grabbed on to the shelf of the hutch. Leaning forward, he placed his foot on the buffet and reached for the bottle. His foot slipped. He wobbled wildly and clutched the top of the hutch.

He flew back and tried to right himself by pulling himself forward. He felt the bump of fright, though his brain wasn't firing on all cylinders. The hutch began to rock forward toward Hobo. The chair rocked wildly and flew out from under Hobo and he fell forward, his face hitting the top of the buffet. The loud melon sound bounced around the small room. The hutch tottered wildly and plates began to fall. Dishes slid and crashed onto the ground. Blood sprayed out and splashed onto wood and dishes. Hobo bounced off the buffet and landed on the wood floor. The heavy oak hutch toppled over, landed on top of Hobo, and knocked him out.

CHAPTER TWENTY-TWO

Robby Rob moved through the dark of the coal mine, sometimes bumping his head on the uneven ceiling. It was near pitch black in the coal mine, the only light coming from several wavering candles placed on ledges and a couple tables. He bumped into a man, Stroh, he thought. It was hard to tell, but thought he recognized the policeman's face. He'd had a run-in or two with the man in the past.

Robby Rob watched the man maneuver around a group of women to stop by a woman with her arm around a little girl. The officer placed his arm around her and kissed her head. Robby Rob shook his head; these pinheads were all trapped down here and no one was willing to try to get the hell out. He'd only been here a day and knew he couldn't stay down here.

Those lunatic white bastards had put him in this hole and told him that if he wanted to live, he had to work. There was no way he was going to work for those crazy crackers. A metal basket was coming down the shaft and he knew food was on its way. He stepped forward and shoved people out of the way.

He reached the basket and was about to grab the food when he felt a hand on his arm. He turned and saw Officer Stroh. He looked down at the man's hand on his arm and looked at the officer.

"You ain't the po po here, Stroh, get your hand off my arm," Robby Rob said, his face leaning in aggressively toward the other man.

"You haven't worked, and if you don't work, you don't eat. We all have to work down here, or they stop feeding us," Stroh said.

"You ain't the boss down here, officer, and I ain't gotta listen to you," Robby Rob snarled and jerked his arm out of Stroh's grasp.

"Yeah, he ain't the boss, but you don't eat, asshole, unless you put in a full day of work down here," said a large black man, the breadth of his chest unreal. The man stepped forward, looming over Robby Rob, his huge ham-like fists resting on his hips.

Robby Rob stepped back and looked around him. There were other men standing around now, glaring at him. Their faces were covered with coal dust and smeared with sweat. He could feel sweat prickling his head and warning bells blaring in his brain.

"Well, why ain't the women and young'uns workin'? Why is they just sittin' around on their asses, doing nothin'?" Robby Rob asked belligerently.

"Are you stupid, boy?" the giant asked him. "This is man's work. Now get your scrawny ass down that tunnel and get to work, or I will beat you to death to save us all the trouble."

Robby Rob was shoved away from the food and pointed in the direction of the dark tunnel. He shoved his hands in his pocket, his brain racing. There was no way he wanted to work as those jackass's slave. But he was hungry, and he knew those men wouldn't let him eat if he didn't work. He'd be damned if he'd let them work him like a mule. Maybe he could steal some food, take it from one of the kids or women. He'd have to think about it.

Ж

They called him Hercules, but David Colman hadn't really minded. David had always been an easy-going man, until he wasn't. It took a lot to get David's temper going, but when it did get going, he was like a freight train and ran over whoever was making him mad.

David had served just one tour in the Army in Afghanistan. That had been enough for him. He'd come back to Beattyville, where he'd grown up. David had been a guard at the First National Bank on Main Street. He'd liked his job because he knew he intimidated people into minding their manners.

The day the power went out, he'd helped lock the bank up and had gone home. His small apartment had been hot, since there was no power for air conditioning. He'd not known what happened but had hoped the power would come back on. He'd been sitting in a beach chair down at the pool with a few other residents. He'd had a beer with him, and everyone was just talking and laughing.

Before anyone realized what was happening, a man had come up behind him and put a shotgun to his head. He'd been taken with another man, who was black as well, and they'd been taken to the coal mine. Along the way, he'd found out that the mayor and sheriff were responsible. David didn't even know how long he'd been down here, as it was always dark.

235

Slowly, other people began arriving in the same way: white and black folks. Everyone's story was the same. Anyone white who tried to help a black or Hispanic was thrown down in the mine as well. David couldn't believe this was going on in the new century. Hadn't they all moved beyond this kind of hate?

He'd heard stories from his father and grandfather, but at the age of thirty, nothing remotely like this had happened to him. Part of the reason was of his size: he was six-foot-six and two hundred ninety pounds. There weren't many that messed with him.

He'd been well liked at work, never a mean word said, or action. He had always been a thoughtful man, and had been raised to be careful because of his size. To have the hate that the men who'd captured him spewed in his direction was so shocking. In the military, there had never been any kind of racist talk. He knew it might have gone on, but, in the military, that got you kicked out. The military didn't put up with that kind of horseshit.

He'd been shocked at seeing women and children brought down. The mine was damp and cool. The air wasn't too bad until you went deeper into the mine to work. There was a pregnant woman, Mary. He'd heard her husband had been a policeman and his own people had murdered him. David shook his head in sorrow. He'd made it his mission to ensure she was kept warm and well-fed. He'd met her neighbor, Gideon, and his family. Gideon told David about how the men had handled Mary.

David walked over to Mary, who was sitting bundled up. He had his helmet on with the light lit, and could see her. She had her mask over her face and he was glad to see it. He knew this air wasn't good for any of them. Deeper in the mine was worse, what with the pockets of gas below.

"They sent some breakfast down. I brought you some peaches, a boiled egg, and a hamburger bun," David said, handing over the food.

Mary smiled up at him and took the food. "Thank you, David. Did you eat something yourself?" she asked.

"I will. I wanted to make sure you had your breakfast first. Gideon is holding some eggs for me and a couple buns. He reached into his coveralls and pulled out a pint of milk. He saw her smile and returned it. "Figured I'd better get you this before they ran out. I'll be heading down to work in a bit. Is there anything I can get you?" David asked

"Oh David, thank you. You're so kind to me. Thank you," Mary said, her mouth trembling and her eyes tearing up.

David reached over and patted her hand with his large one. "Mary, it's nothing. We have to take care of each other. We'll make it out of here, somehow, some way. You just stay healthy for you and your baby." He stood up.

"Thank you again, David. You'll never know what it means to me and my baby, that you are here for us, you and Gideon and his family. It makes all this bearable," Mary said, her voice soft.

237

"We only have each other down here. We have to stick together. Get some rest if you can," David said, and turned away, going to find Gideon and his breakfast.

He was worried about Mary. If she had the baby down here, he was sure it wouldn't survive. He and Gideon had been brainstorming, trying to think of a way to get a message out and to someone who'd help them. So far, nothing had come to mind.

He joined Gideon and took his breakfast, popping an egg into his mouth. He was so hungry all the time. He knew he was losing weight. There were many mouths to feed, and he couldn't bring himself to steal from another just to feel full. If things didn't get better soon, people, especially the women and children, were going to start dying. David suspected that was their plan all along.

Ж

Harry had just come in from chopping wood. Though it was mid-summer, winter wasn't that far off, and with no electricity, they'd need the wood for keeping the house warm and cooking. Willene didn't want to use the propane during the winter. At least using the cook stove would also help heat the house.

The farmhouse was large, with four bedrooms on the second story and two smaller bedrooms on the first floor. The rooms on the second story always stayed warm in the winter, as the heat from the fireplace in the living room rose to them.

Earl was sitting on the swing on the porch with Monroe, snapping beans for Willene. She was going to make beans and potatoes with fried cornbread cakes for dinner, along with sliced tomatoes and fried rabbit that Boggy had caught this morning. Clay was in the rocking chair, having been helped there by Harry earlier.

Katie was on watch. She was currently walking the perimeter; he'd seen her up past the chicken lot. He nodded to Clay and Earl, and patted Monroe on the head. Both dogs were asleep, Brian asleep at Clay's feet. It was late afternoon, and the day was winding down. Marilyn had been working in the garden most of the day with Monroe, pulling weeds and picking beans and some tomatoes. It would be canning time soon.

"Where are my beans?" Willene yelled through the house from the kitchen.

"You better take this mess of beans inside before she skins our tails. She's awaitin' on them," Earl said, laughing, nudging the little boy. Monroe grinned a big gap-toothed grin, hopped off the swing, and took the bowl from Earl. Harry opened the screen door for the child and Monroe disappeared into the house.

Harry sat beside Earl on the swing and brought out his pipe and lit it, puffing away until the bowl glowed. Boggy was out in the chicken lot gathering eggs and feeding the chickens. Harry looked over when he heard Marilyn coming from the kitchen, carrying a tray of sun tea and glasses. Harry jumped up and went to the screen door, holding it open for her. He smiled down at her, his eyes triangled with humor.

"Thanks Harry, take a glass and pour you some," Marilyn said, looking up and returning his smile.

He noticed she blushed a little, and he grinned bigger. "Sure. Can I help with dinner?"

"Oh Lord, no, Willy told me how you are in the kitchen," she said and laughed.

Harry rolled his eyes, took a glass and filled it. He handed it to Clay, then filled one for Earl and one for himself. Katie came around the corner, the AR-15 in her hands. Willene had given her a few lessons in using the AR-15, though they couldn't fire the weapon for fear of others knowing what they had. Willene had told him that she'd picked up fast on the training, and that she had a willingness to learn and defend them. Katie had insisted on being added to the watch rotation.

"Come on and take a seat and rest for a few," Harry said. He took a glass, filled it with tea, and handed it to her. She smiled up at him and took the proffered glass, then went over to sit by Clay and sipped.

Marilyn headed back into the house as Monroe ran back out onto the porch. He went to Earl, who pulled the boy onto his lap. Harry smiled softly. Monroe was becoming very attached to Earl. He reached over and patted the child's head once more, then grinned at Earl, who returned the grin.

There was a cool breeze blowing up the hill, the pungent fug of smoke riding on it. Though no one could see fires, they were there and had been going for over a week. No one spoke, enjoying the silence and the creaking of the swing and rockers. In the far distance, he heard a bobwhite calling. It was times like this that all was well with the world, even this new world. Deep in the trees, he could see lightning bugs starting to glow.

Harry looked up and down the road below; he liked the high vantage the house gave, here on the porch it was nearly a panoramic view. From his bedroom, he had an even better view. He kept his bedroom door locked since his rifle was permanently set up on a tripod pointed down the hill. He rocked slowly in the swing, and lifted his head when he spotted Alan's truck coming down the road, heading toward the house. He got up and walked to the edge of the porch.

"Looks like Alan is coming to pay us a visit. I'll meet him down there," Harry said, and left the porch, heading down the hill at an easy gait.

By the time Harry got down the hill, the truck was coming to a stop about fifty yards up the road. He squeezed through the barricade and walked toward the truck. He was shocked when Alan got out of the truck: the boy's face was red, his eyes puffy from crying. The boy walked around the truck and opened the passenger-side door. He reached in and pulled something out.

When Alan came around the truck, he was carrying a car seat with a baby strapped in. Harry was shocked and concerned. He walked quickly to the boy and took the car seat from Alan. He placed his arm around the thin teen's shoulders and walked the boy to the house. The teen couldn't speak, simply cried hard all the way.

Katie got up and called Willene, who came out onto the porch. She walked over to Alan and put her arm around him, then walked him over to the glider. Alan had started to cry even harder, and Harry handed over a clean handkerchief. The boy took it and brought it to his face, and tried to stifle the weeping.

"My math teacher, Mr. Santo, and his wife an' their son, Robert, was hung. Someone hung my friend. He's only fifteen, he was younger than me," Alan cried out, rocking back and forth, Katie rubbing his back. Everyone sucked in their breath at the shocking revelation.

Willene took the baby from the car seat and held the child to her chest. She turned and went back into the kitchen.

"I found this letter pinned to his momma's dress. Just read it," Alan said, handing over the wadded piece of paper. Harry took it and read it aloud.

These Mexicans have polluted our town. Any Mexicans found will be treated the same. Only white people can come to our town. Stay the hell out or you die like these Mexicans.

Alan's face was painted in pale freckles, and his large square teeth bit into his lower lip. The soft down on his face met with the sporadic stubble on his chin, his face caving in on itself with grief. His short hair stood on end where he'd pulled on it in stress.

"They ain't Mexicans, they was Puerto Rican and they're Americans like us," he said and cried harder, and Katie pulled the lanky boy into her arms and held him. Harry could see the boy was badly shaken. He shook his head. His heart broke for the kid and the family.

"That's his little sister, Angela. They called her Angel, cause she's so sweet," Alan said. He wiped his

242

nose on the handkerchief, and then dug in his pocket. "I found this notice in town. I seen a bunch of 'em around town. I reckon you should see em," Alan said and handed the paper to Harry.

Harry looked at the paper, then read it out loud, *"Notice to all, there is a bounty on any non-white and non-Christian persons or families. Bring anyone who fits this description to the sheriff's office and you will be paid in food and goods. Anyone helping these undesirables will be rounded up and put in jail. Penalties may include servitude or death. This town will not tolerate deception or hiding or protecting these people."*

Harry's lip curled in disgust and anger.

"What is wrong with these people?" Marilyn asked, holding Monroe in her arms as she stood by the screen door.

"Evil, that's what they are. Lord have mercy, just evil," Katie said, shaking her head. She looked round at the group through tear-filled eyes.

"There must be something we can do," Clay said, anger and grief lacing his voice.

"I don't know. I wish I did," Harry said. He was frustrated, with no clear way to go. He felt like his hands were tied.

"I heard from some of my neighbors that they'd been puttin' everyone and anyone in that coal mine. Women an' young'uns too, they have been puttin' whole families down them holes. And anyone who's helpin', they end up there too," Alan said.

"Them mines ain't no place for young'uns an' women. That coal dust gets everywhere. It is dark as hell itself," Boggy said, wiping his face with both his hands.

"I'd just soon be in hell with my back broke than go back ta that mine," Earl said, shaking his head.

"It's a hard place for certain," Boggy agreed.

"I gotta get back home, and I can't come back cause I ain't got much gas left, and if I can find some gas, I'll be back and I'm gonna take down Mr. and Mrs. Santo and Robert, an I'll bury them," Alan said.

"Alan, can you do me a favor? It will be dangerous, so listen to what I have to say before you say yes," Harry said. He could feel all eyes on him.

"Sure, Harry. What is it?" Alan asked.

Harry hated to do this, but their situation was intolerable. He hated asking Alan to help, because he was still a child in his eyes. Yet, Alan might be their key. Alan might be their only hope. Would the boy be brave enough? Was it right of him to ask the teen? If he didn't, then all could be lost. Perhaps with a little help from their friends, they might just find a way to survive and then win against the overwhelming odds they faced. Only time would tell and with Alan's assistance.

Made in the USA
Monee, IL
10 November 2023

46203548R00134